EARLY PRAISE FOR EMERGENCE

"Shiloah excels at character development... Along with convincing dramatic moments, Shiloah writes astute and occasionally exhilarating hospital scenes that readers unfamiliar with medical jargon will effortlessly follow."

—*Kirkus*

"Anesthesiologist Shira Shiloah takes an almost unthinkable premise and weaves a haunting tale. A scalpel-wielding villain, a failed health care system, and a whistleblower that protects her patients. With unexpected twists and satisfying drama, a neurosurgeon casually cuts and kills patients in a modern-day Memphis hospital. You'll never look at your own surgeon the same way."

—Robert Dugoni,
New York Times and
#1 Amazon bestselling author

"...creating a tantalizing plot for fans who like their happily-ever-after with a dash of medical malice."

—*BookLife*

"We all face major surgery sooner or later, and our calculus in submitting to it begins with the competence and wisdom of the surgeon. Do we trust him or her? We'd better, but how can we be sure? Shira Shiloah, in her striking first novel, will give you something to think about as you schedule that hip or knee replacement. Suppose the surgeon comes across as entirely plausible but isn't right in the head? Suppose his antic demons often run away with him? The author is herself a doctor, and she packs *Emergence* with a realism gained firsthand. Come join Roxanne Roth, an anesthesiologist at a Memphis hospital, as she realizes that, incredibly, she's working in the OR alongside a killer. *Emergence* is an unusual and first-rate thriller."

—John Hough, Jr,
author of *Little Bighorn* and *Seen the Glory:
A Novel of the Battle of Gettysburg.*

"Dr. Shira Shiloah draws from her medical insight and experience to take the reader on a thriller journey behind the locked doors of operating rooms and clinics. While accurately describing the space and procedures of medicine, she adds the personalities and actions of the health care workers caring for patients, proving that they are human and experience the same challenges of life as all.

In the process, we meet a surgeon, caught between performing surgeries and attempting to accommodate an insatiable desire for drugs, while being challenged by a doctor upholding her morals and insisting on the best medical care possible."

—Henry Jay Przybylo, MD, MFA,
and author of *Counting Backwards.*

EMERGENCE

by

Shira Shiloah, MD

EMERGENCE: A novel
Copyright © Shira Shiloah

HARDBACK ISBN 978-1-7351930-2-1
PAPERBACK ISBN 978-1-7351930-0-7
AUDIOBOOK ISBN 978-1-7351930-3-8
EBOOK ISBN 978-1-7351930-1-4

Published by Salty Air Publishing, Memphis, Tennessee

Publisher's Cataloging-In-Publication Data

Names: Shiloah, Shira, author.
Title: Emergence / Shira Shiloah, MD.
Description: Memphis, Tennessee : Salty Air Publishing, [2020]
Identifiers: ISBN 9781735193021 (Hardback) | ISBN 9781735193007 (Paperback) |
    ISBN 9781735193014 (Ebook)
Subjects: LCSH: Neurosurgeons—Fiction. | Widows—Fiction. | Anesthesiologists—
    Fiction. | Psychopaths—Fiction. |
    Murder—Fiction. | LCGFT: Medical fiction. | Thrillers (fiction)
Classification: LCC PS3619.H55 E44 2020 (print) | LCC PS3619.H55 (ebook) |
    DDC 813/.6—dc23

Cover Design by James T. Egan
Book Interior and E-book Design by Amit Dey
Copy Edited by Ericka McIntyre
Proofread by Cassandra Lipp

In loving memory of Paula, Jon,
and my beautiful cousins, Dana and Ronit

CHAPTER ONE

⌒

*A*s Dr. D.K. Webb walked out of the hospital at noon, the surge of power he'd felt using just the tips of his fingers still coursed through him, as did euphoria. He'd twisted the pedicle screw into the exact spot along her spine, confirming with X-ray that she'd wake up a different woman because of his work. Got another one, he thought, as he mounted his motorcycle.

He revved up his customized P-51 Combat Fighter, a motorcycle built from aircraft-grade futuristic aluminum, and sold for the median cost of a local home. The level of menace underneath him echoed his mood as he weaved through the sparse weekend traffic, his license plate *MD4SPINE* a blur to the occasional cars he passed. Gun it and run it, he thought.

Crystal greeted him wearing nothing but a white thong and a smile when he walked into the apartment. He kissed her, biting her lower lip; her endless legs wrapped around his waist as he carried her past the dirty dishes and empty beer bottles on the coffee table to his unmade king bed. She laughed with her arms outstretched to him as her bottom hit the mattress.

"No laughing, this is serious business," he said, and kissed her generous familiar lips. Her ebony skin smelled of coconut moisturizer as he buried his head between her breasts. His lips found her left nipple ring before his head moved in between her thighs. Afterward, they fell asleep in each other's arms, his right arm over her waist. When they awoke the room had darkened. She kissed him and got dressed by the bed, inching into a black dress that clung to every curve.

"Don't go." He bounded out of bed and his six-foot-four frame pinned her arms against the wall. He bent down to nuzzle her slender neck, his soft platinum hair against her. "Come on baby, spend the night, spread those legs for me again."

"I've gotta work, you gorgeous man. I'll stay next time, I promise." She kissed his forehead. "You go have fun tonight."

When he walked her out of his downtown apartment he felt cooler air against his pale face. It was the first break in the humid summer heat of Memphis and his polo shirt wasn't drenched in sweat, for a change. He navigated over the South Main Trolley's train tracks once it rumbled past and caught a glance of the Bass Pro sign on the Memphis pyramid. He took The Peabody hotel's elevator to the rooftop, and nodded a sign of recognition to the bouncer as he passed him. Among the white sorority girl cliques in stilettos, he spotted a solo blonde at a high top table. She stood aligned in four-inch heels, a woman who'd never suffered from back pain, or perhaps any pain. She was busying herself with the decorative carnations on the table, her manicured fingers rearranging them to her liking. Her hair, even lighter than his, was pulled into a high ponytail, and she wore red lips and cat-like eyeliner. Her skirt was how he liked it too, nice and short; she had the toned, limber legs of the Ole Miss cheerleaders he used to bang. *Rah Rah Rah*. Even though she was youthful, her face showed the beginning of crow's feet. This girl liked to party, he thought. The Harahan Bridge wouldn't be the only thing getting lit tonight.

"One dirty martini and a white wine." He flashed his blue eyes at the petite bartender. His particular brand of Scandinavian good looks opened doors and women easily. With drinks in hand, he strode over to his mark. Holding out the wine glass he said, "If I offered you a drink, would your husband kill me?"

Her glance was emotionless. "I'm no wifey."

"Lucky me, then." He stepped closer. "Would you consider celebrating with me?"

The woman took the offered glass from his hand as her gaze fell onto him, taking in his clean-shaven face with the slight overbite, his broad shoulders, and his Rolex watch. With her heels, he was just a few inches taller than her. His long fingers were free of any wedding band.

"So what're you celebrating?" She sipped the wine. "Are you overjoyed this ancient bridge is lighting up?"

"Not quite." He finished his glass in two sips. "A difficult case went well today."

"You a lawyer?"

"Neurosurgeon." He put his glass down on the table and saw a faint smile appear on her full lips. This is going to be so easy, he thought. Not as easy as paying Crystal, but he liked an occasional freebie.

When she started talking about her job as a sales rep, he focused on her lips until he spotted a stunning brunette across the rooftop. Roxanne Roth. His medical school classmate's long dark hair was down; she wore a fitted red sweater and was talking to a man with a diamond earring and tattoos. She had gotten even hotter, he thought. When she glanced in his direction, he winked at her. Roxanne waved and turned back to the guy she was with. Since when did a piece like Roxanne Roth slum it, he thought.

His phone vibrated. It was the surgical intensive care unit calling, again. He put it on silent and slipped it back inside his jeans front pocket. The sunset had created a red glow above the mighty Mississippi River. He saw the beauty as proof of his invincibility; like the weather, he was unstoppable.

CHAPTER TWO

Dr. Roxanne Roth had issues, none of which she could attend to right now. Instead, she focused on the patient in front of her. She placed her hands on the sides of his neck and palpated for hard lumps. The fact that she couldn't feel any was a reassuring sign the golf-ball-sized tumor on the side of his tongue hadn't spread.

The preoperative holding room was filled with eight other patients on stretchers with flimsy curtains separating them from one another. The harsh fluorescent lighting above them added to the intrusive environment they found themselves in. No longer individuals with pockets and shoes, they were naked patients wearing hospital gowns. Although Roxanne spoke in a soft voice to offer a degree of privacy, her patient gave minimal eye contact.

"Maybe I can address some of your questions, Anthony," she said, adjusting her silver-rimmed glasses on the bridge of her nose. "What are you most concerned about?"

"Of losing my tongue." His voice cracked as he rubbed the top of his balding head. "I'm afraid of never eating again. Of dying from this cancer."

"Of course you're frightened," she said as she reached behind him. She handed him a box of tissues from the top shelf behind his stretcher.

"I should've gone to the doctor sooner." He pulled a tissue from the box she held and blotted his eyes.

"What's important is that you're here now. I'll be watching over you the entire surgery and Dr. Armstrong's excellent. He's the chair of the department for a reason."

Dr. Brian Armstrong approached them with a pen in hand and picked up Anthony's chart from the foot of the bed. He flipped through it, signed the surgical consent, and put his pen in his coat pocket before making eye contact with them both. "Dr. Roth, ready to roll?"

Roxanne patted the patient's hand and said, "I'll be back in a few minutes."

She turned her back to Anthony and tossed Brian an upside-down smile. By lightly tugging on his lab coat sleeve, she led him to the nurse's station, away from the patient's listening range.

"Do you have to be so rude?" she said. "The poor guy's terrified."

"Was I rude? I'm just short on time." He checked his wristwatch. "I was hoping we could roll back early."

She stared at him while tilting her head, making her ponytail bounce. "Show no fear," a lesson Roxanne learned early in residency, had served her well over the years. "It's not even seven-fifteen," she said. "And there's nothing you can say to make me work faster than I already do. There *is*, however, a lot you could say right now to make me slow down."

He held his palms up. "Forgive me, clearly I forgot who I was working with."

"You go reassure our patient. I vouched for you," she said. "I'll pick up narcs and then we'll roll, *early*, your majesty."

Roxanne was relieved to find the recovery room empty. She could handle her surgeon, but wasn't ready to face a certain recovery room nurse. She logged onto the computerized drug dispenser, chose narcotics, and then walked back to pre-op while pulling a blue bouffant cap out of the back pocket of her hospital-issued scrubs. She tucked her dark hair into it knowing a curl or two would inevitably escape.

Liz, the operating room circulating nurse, was speaking with Anthony. Liz had a neck tattoo of three small blackbirds in various stages of flight, at least four piercings in each ear, and a piercing in her eyebrow and nose. Roxanne noticed the outline of a cigarette box in the back pocket of Liz's fitted black scrubs. She would scold her about that later.

"Anthony, you've got the best surgeon *and* the best nurse. Here comes some medicine," Roxanne said as she injected the drug midazolam into his IV. She rubbed his arm gently over the IV site. "Sometimes this medicine stings a bit. Can you start thinking of somewhere you vacation?"

Midazolam was Roxanne's favorite anesthetic since it enabled her to give Anthony a more calming experience. She would get him through his ordeal with the right combination of drugs and skill. Anthony relaxed his head back into the pillow.

"Pickwick," he said, with droopy eyelids.

"You fish there?" Roxanne motioned to Liz who pulled at the stretcher near Anthony's feet, while Roxanne pushed at the head of the bed. It hurt her back a little, an occupational hazard she hadn't been warned about in medical school. They passed by two other patients on stretchers before entering the hallway. As they passed operating room number nine, Roxanne momentarily closed her eyes.

"I'll go out on our Galati cruiser from dawn 'til nightfall," Anthony said.

Outside operating suite eleven, Roxanne stopped to pull her scrub mask out of the back pocket of her scrubs. She tied it behind her head and then pushed the stretcher inside. The tech, in sterile gown and gloves, was inside arranging her surgical instruments on a Mayo stand. Roxanne caught a whiff of ammonia from the linoleum floor and shivered as the air-conditioning blew above her. She sneezed into her mask.

"Bless you." A male voice from inside the room. Roxanne glanced to find his six-foot frame. Resident doctor Justin Kirkland was going to scrub in on the case.

"Thanks," she said quietly, her gaze darted to the anesthesia machine, anywhere Justin wasn't. His thick dark hair was covered in a scrub hat and though his surgical mask was on, she imagined his lopsided smile and ever-present five o'clock shadow. He sat on a stool by the computer workstation and his arms rested on his knees, watching her. Roxanne felt her face redden. She pulled her surgical mask higher, wishing she'd woken earlier to apply eye makeup.

Roxanne pulled the stretcher close to the operating table, stepped on a lever at the head to lock it in place, and patted the surface. "Anthony, stay on your back and scoot over here." Her faint southern drawl became obvious with the word "here." Once his monitors were on, Roxanne placed a plastic mask lightly over his nose and mouth. "This smells like a new shower curtain. I'm going to get you off to sleep." She glanced at the screen on the machine and confirmed that his heart rate, blood pressure, and oxygen saturation were normal. And when he took a breath, she was reassured that the green waveform of carbon dioxide was visible on the screen.

"You might feel medicine burn in your IV again. You keep dreaming, catch a fish for me. We're going to take good care of you." The midazolam had taken full effect on Anthony, and his eyes were closed.

"I trust you," he said.

She knew her patients took this leap of faith every day; that when they leapt, she would catch. So far, she hadn't broken her word.

CHAPTER THREE

Roxanne pushed propofol, its milky appearance resembling a piña colada, into the IV while reassuring her patient with what Liz dubbed her "Momma Roth" voice.

"You're doing great," she said.

"Thank you for..." Anthony said.

Roxanne wondered if those were the last comprehensible words he'd ever speak. Would he wake up missing most of his tongue?

A moment later he lost consciousness as well as the ability to breathe. Roxanne needed to secure a breathing tube, but when she tried to fill his lungs with oxygen using the mask and bag of her usual routine, she couldn't. His tumor was obstructive. She heard the oxygen saturation monitor pitch change from high to low, a dreaded sound in her line of work.

"Liz, pull the difficult airway cart closer, I'm not moving any air." Roxanne said as she pushed an oral airway into Anthony's mouth to force his diseased tongue out of the way.

Justin hopped off his chair. "What can I do?"

"Man the bag."

Justin stood behind her and squeezed the bag of the anesthesia circuit while Roxanne used both of her hands to thrust Anthony's jaw up and seal the face mask onto him with her thumbs. The oxygen saturation monitor alarmed now, his oxygen saturation read sixty, and his lips were turning blue. They still weren't getting oxygen into his lungs.

"Liz, call stat back up!" Roxanne reached for an LMA. She took out the useless oral airway and in one motion replaced it with the larger and more secure LMA. She saw her patient's chest rise and fall and the carbon dioxide monitor showed a tracing of his breath. After a few tense seconds the oxygen monitor returned to its higher pitch and Anthony's lips went from blue to pink.

"Anesthesia stat OR eleven!" A woman's voice blasted from the ceiling speakers.

"We're stable," Roxanne said, waving her hand. "Liz, cancel the code."

She gave Anthony another minute of one hundred percent oxygen as she slowed her own breath. "I'm going to take one look. If it's not easy, I'll wake him."

"Got it," said Justin.

She took out the LMA and rapidly placed a breathing tube into Anthony's right nostril. She put a fiberoptic blade in his mouth and felt relieved she could see vocal cords. She slid the breathing tube into his trachea. She listened for breath sounds on both sides, taped the tube in place, and turned up the anesthesia gas.

Justin moved to the side of her. She was well aware of all of his movements. "Well done, doctor," he said.

She covered her patient's eyes with tape, afraid to lift her own. "Thanks for the assist."

"So you been up to anything fun besides managing airways?" he said.

"You call this fun?" She tucked a loose curl back into her cap. "I went to Brooklyn a couple of weeks ago, visited friends from residency. Had way too much sushi and pizza."

"I can't remember my last vacation."

"Well, I'm not a resident anymore. It gets a lot better." She cleared her throat. "Or is it your girlfriend that saps your time?"

"Girlfriend? I wish. All the good girls are taken."

She was either a bad girl or Justin thought she was taken. After her one-night stand with Nick on Saturday, she considered she might be the former.

Dr. Armstrong walked into the operating room while texting on his cell phone. "Roxanne, could you give ten of decadron, please?"

"Already have," she said. "And you missed a difficult ventilation, 'Doctor I'm in a hurry.'"

"Everyone said you handled it." Dr. Armstrong put his phone on Liz's computer work station. "Okay, I'm completely present. Let's scrub, Justin."

Roxanne sat behind the blue sterile sheet, referred to in the anesthesia community as "the blood/brain barrier"—surgeons stood on the bloody side while they were the intellectual side. She listened to Justin and Brian as they worked. "Did you watch the Cubbies clinch the National division?" Justin said. "Can't believe it's them and the Indians in a World Series."

"You did med school in Chicago, right?" Brian held a scalpel against Anthony's tongue.

⌒

"Call path?" Brian said, once the tumor was extracted. Liz picked up the phone. "We're ready for the pathologist in OR 11," she said. She took a six-ounce clear plastic cup out of the cabinet, opened it, and held it above the blue field. Dr. Armstrong held the tumor with sterile metal forceps and released it into the container. Liz peeled a patient label from Anthony's chart, stuck it to the top of the container, and screwed the lid shut. Moments later the pathologist shuffled into the operating room as if he were there to change a light bulb, not predict life expectancy.

"This is a squamous cell cancer from biopsy and the left suture's superior. I need to know if all the margins are free before I close up," Dr. Armstrong said.

Dr. Peterson, with curly gray hair peeking out of his surgical cap, said, "Yeah, got it." He took the specimen, tore a billing sheet from the chart, and headed to the lab adjacent to the operating suites.

"So what's your prediction, Brian?" said Roxanne. "He'll need a trach?"

"I think we got it all. I might send some lymph nodes for frozen section but I'm hoping we're done. Really depends what path says."

"Music okay?" Liz said and turned on the radio. Maroon 5's "Sugar" played. As the surgeons stood, gowned and gloved under the hot operating lights, Brian folded his hands and rocked back and forth on his heels while

Justin tapped his fingers to the beat on the metal tray. Justin's gaze wandered over to Roxanne, who was seated by the anesthesia machine with a hot blanket wrapped around her. She avoided eye contact, obsessing about the "good girls taken" comment. Was she on his radar as a potential? Not that it mattered. She wasn't in the market for any more heartbreak.

Anthony lay with the breathing tube through his nose, his arms tucked to his sides. His heart monitor was audible over the music. She noticed his blood pressure had lowered a bit so she reduced the anesthesia gas. When Dr. Peterson called into the operating room, Liz put him on speakerphone and turned off the radio.

Roxanne prayed silently for Anthony. Her prayers weren't often answered, but it didn't stop her from trying.

Peterson's voice boomed over the speakerphone: "Squamous cell, margins clear."

And there it was. The cancer was contained. Roxanne's surgical mask hid her smile. Anthony would talk again; he would eat again. He would have only a small part of his tongue removed and not need a tracheostomy.

Once the surgeons finished up, Roxanne awoke Anthony from anesthesia as carefully as she could. She hoped she'd given him the right amount of pain medicine so he wouldn't bite down, tear his incisions and bleed. Blood in his now-swollen airway would be an absolute disaster.

CHAPTER FOUR

⌒

A s Anthony emerged without disturbance, Roxanne removed the breathing tube and gave oxygen through the face mask she held gently over his incisions. She'd chosen a high-risk art as her life's work; induce a coma and then pull someone out of it, on time and without pain. It took training, vigilance, and a little bit of madness when she really thought about it. Her residency had replaced her fear of killing someone with confidence; now that she was trained, taking people to the brink of death then pulling them back had become her daily routine. She only wished she could've pulled Mark back out of his surgery. She hadn't been given a chance to save her fiancé who died two doors down in nine. To her, that operating room was his coffin. Her partners understood she couldn't do cases there, and without any explanation required, switched her out of it when necessary.

"Does every guy wake up blissed out with you?" Justin said, beside her again. Roxanne cleared her throat. She could not process Justin. He was a disturbance in her life. He wasn't supposed to be taking up any residence in her head and definitely not in her heart. Yet she couldn't deny the excitement she felt when he noticed her, when he spoke to her. He was four years her junior but she felt like a jittery teenager near him.

"Are you...?" she said. "Are you wanting inside information? I'm not sure..."

"Code OR sixteen," a woman's voice came blasting from the ceiling speakers. Roxanne watched the back of Justin's muscular frame as he bolted out the door. Both the moment, and the case, were over.

Liz and Roxanne helped Anthony move back onto his stretcher. As they pushed the stretcher into recovery, waiting to receive them was Nurse Nick.

Damn it, Roxanne thought.

Nick's cropped black hair framed a face with full lips and a close-trimmed goatee. He wore a diamond stud in his right ear. An image of him naked flashed in her mind. His tattoos covered his extensive canvas of muscles; seared in her memory was his shoulder tattoo—a wolf's head in black and white, teeth bared. She remembered kissing it when he was on top of her.

She hadn't *planned* on seeing him naked, she reasoned. Her neighbors, other young professionals living in her downtown loft condominium building, convinced her to take a break from studying for her anesthesiology oral board exam and join them for a rooftop party to watch the historic lighting of the Harahan Bridge. She knew friendship with her neighbors was a good idea, but she really preferred to study.

When they'd entered The Peabody hotel's roof deck she saw people milling around with cocktails and mini sandwiches on paper napkins. A band of four musicians was warming up and she heard a lot of feedback from the guitar. It was cooler out and she was comfortable in her red sweater and knee-high black leather boots, her fitted jeans tucked into them. The sun had set on the Mississippi River and the sky, orange and yellow with pink clouds. It reminded her of Mark. Most beautiful things did.

She saw Nick make a beeline for her, with a grin on his face and a beer in his hand.

"Hey it's hot Dr. Roth all dressed up," he'd said. "I don't recognize you with real clothes on."

"Hey," she'd said. Without a hair bonnet and sterile mask, co-workers often didn't recognize her, nor did she recognize them. Now she wished her pants were as form fitting. "Just wanted to see the fireworks."

"Come watch them with me, doc." He started to pull her toward the veranda. The band started playing.

She pulled back, her outstretched arm straight, causing him to stop.

"I'm with friends." She tilted her head toward the bar. Her neighbors smiled at him.

"Oh, I mean no offense. Would you like to watch the fireworks with me? Please? We never hang outside of work."

She acquiesced, enjoying his strong hand against the small of her back, imagining it was Mark's hand. It had been so long since she'd allowed herself to be held. And Nick was as easy on the eyes as he was warm on the skin.

"Tequila or whiskey?" A younger woman in a crop top and shorts approached them, holding up two shot glasses.

"Shot?" Nick said, taking his wallet out of his back pocket.

"Sure. Whiskey." Why not, she thought. It's not like the anesthesia oral boards were tomorrow. She had over eight months to practice.

They clinked their glasses together and slung them back. The cold fluid burned in her throat and she coughed, covering her mouth. When she glanced back up she saw her old medical school classmate D.K. "Dickie" Webb across the deck. It looked like things hadn't changed much for him; he was still extraordinarily handsome and the blonde next to him looked barely legal. Roxanne heard he'd become neurosurgery staff, and she gave a polite wave when he winked at her.

One drink. Fireworks. Then another drink. The Harahan Bridge, which spanned the Mississippi River from Tennessee to Arkansas, lit up with a rainbow of colors. Memphis looked glamorous, she thought. Another drink. Nick pulled her into a slow dance, more of a hug than a dance really, followed by laughs and longer hugs until she felt him kiss her cheek. And her mouth. He tasted good, his kisses were hungry and hers were too.

"You want to walk me home?" she said, surprising even herself.

"I'll walk anywhere you want," he said.

When they stumbled into her condo her dog, Lyla, greeted them with excited whimpers. "Go to the couch, Lyla," she said, and petted the top of her head. "Go."

He whispered in Roxanne's ear, his breath smelling of alcohol, "Get you another drink doc or would you prefer I take your clothes off?" He held his left hand firmly on her hip as he unzipped her black jeans. She'd pushed against him, full of desire, kissing him.

Lying in her bed, he'd pulled her boots and then jeans off. "Oh god, you're not wearing panties." She tried to explain her lack of panties, that the pants were too tight to not show the outline but instead she came loudly to his tongue. It felt so good. Then she felt him inside her. It had been so long, and she moved into it, feeling the formidable weight of his body on top of her. But then, it didn't feel good. It felt like betrayal. She let him finish and then cried herself silently to sleep with her back to him once he slept.

⌒

The morning light streamed into her condo, waking her since she had not lowered the blackout drapes in her evening stupor. She felt the fireworks she'd seen had migrated into her head to continue their explosions.

Nick opened his eyes and rolled toward her as if to spoon. "Morning there, hot doc—ready for another round?" he said, the evidence he was indeed up for it rubbed against her.

"I've got to walk my dog. I don't want her to have an accident." She said, extracting herself from his touch. She inch crawled out of her bed, embarrassed by her nakedness, and grabbed the green silk robe from the bench at the foot of the bed. She darted into the master bathroom, shutting the door and locking it behind her. She turned on the shower but sat on the edge of the tub and held her head in her hands. *How am I going to get him out of here?*

She heard a belt being buckled, car keys jingled. Her dog barked. A door slammed. Roxanne turned off the shower and walked out of the bathroom. "Nick?"

He was gone.

I'm never drinking again.

⌒

In the recovery room, after Anthony's surgery, Roxanne struggled not to blush when she saw Nick. She channeled her inner bad girl and composed herself.

"Hey Nick, good morning. Our patient's been very stable, I gave him some atropine since his heart rate runs in the forties. Airway's pretty swollen so I ordered an ICU bed, but it's not ready."

Nick tucked a pen into his scrub shirt pocket. Long gray sleeves covered his tattoos. He placed heart monitors on Anthony and said, "So you need me to babysit him until the unit can take him? You couldn't have ordered a bed earlier and taken him directly there?"

Liz raised her pierced eyebrow at Roxanne and said to Nick, "Dude, don't be rude to Momma Roth."

"I got it, Liz, but thanks for the support."

After Liz gathered her chart and left, Roxanne said, "I did actually order the bed this morning, they're just full." She looked over her anesthesia charting one last time and wrote down the latest vital signs.

Nick's gaze remained fixed on her. "So, did you have a nice weekend, doctor?"

"Yes." She looked him in the eyes. "I had a lovely weekend. And you?"

"I've had better."

Ditto. Much better.

CHAPTER FIVE

Roxanne drove home from the hospital later that day with her right hand on the wheel and her left hand caressing the Tiffany silver heart locket around her neck. The photo inside was a miniaturized picture of her and Mark. Her index finger traced the back of it, the raised cursive engraving she'd touched a thousand times: "All my love, always." She punched the gas of her Camry. He was in a grave. That was the only "always" that was for certain.

It was the one piece of jewelry he'd given her she still wore. In fact, she never took it off, but the engagement ring was in a safe deposit box at her bank. When she moved back to Memphis to be near her family after residency in New York, the memories of their life together in medical school would slice her indiscriminately. During the four years of excruciating work weeks in New York, all she'd focused on was her job; she learned how to care for others while neglecting her own mental health. And no one there knew Mark. But now, back in Memphis, she had to pass their old apartment, their favorite late-night Mexican restaurant where they'd pulled all-nighters studying for gross anatomy, and the student center where they'd worked out in the early mornings. The pain resurfaced like a knife jutting into her and she had no place to hide, no avenue to release her grief.

Her sister, Claire, pestered Roxanne to attend grief counseling. The silver-haired therapist with a gentle voice and warm hands would encourage the old adage, "Approach. Don't avoid. You must walk through the pain to get to a place of peace."

Roxanne did as instructed. She visited Mark's parents and embraced them. His mom was permanently displaced, an empty shell of the strong happy woman she used to be. She'd lost all the joy from her eyes in what Roxanne had learned in her psychiatry course was "complicated grief." His parents' home was filled with pictures of him on the mantle, side tables, and walls. His childhood room remained exactly as he'd left it, only dusted and vacuumed, preserved like a museum. Five years had passed yet his mom lit candles in his memory daily. Roxanne didn't want to become like her, frozen in grief. She wanted to heal.

So if she heard a song that made her want to cry, she allowed herself to, even if she was at cycling class. She went to the coffee house where they'd studied in medical school and memorized cases for her oral board exam, while sipping a chai no water extra cinnamon latte, his drink. She drank it while wiping away tears, but she did it none the less. What she refused to do was visit the grave. Working in the operating suites where he died was torture enough.

The therapist also suggested a dog, and Roxanne would comb through hundreds of Petfinder.com ads when one Saturday a black Cocker Spaniel popped onto the screen. She knew that was her dog. She read the ad and enlarged the pictures.

Lyla. Urgent. She'd been rescued as a stray from the street, no collar, no microchip, and taken to an animal shelter in Mississippi. Under her picture, an ominous message put Roxanne into motion:

This shelter euthanizes dogs that are not claimed after one month.
Sooner if our kennels are full.

Lyla had been in her third week of homelessness when Roxanne drove the hour into Mississippi to rescue her. Lyla had returned the favor with snuggles and kisses ever since, relentlessly so when Roxanne was tearful.

As Roxanne pulled onto her street, drained from her stressful morning with Anthony, two fire trucks and multiple police cars were parked in front of her building. Her neighbors were huddled together, talking and watching, some were not wearing shoes and a woman she didn't know wore a robe, her hair wrapped in a bath towel. She followed their collective gaze. Smoke was coming from the top, her floor.

Lyla!

Police cars had blocked the garage, so she double-parked and bolted for the building's entrance. A massive man, wearing full firefighting gear, extended his arm out. "Wait wait wait lady," he said. "You cannot go in. We've got an active fire."

"My dog's in there. I've got to get her," she said. "Let me in!"

"Shit." The man signaled to one of the policemen controlling the crowd across the street. "Which unit's yours?"

"PH10," she said. "Which unit is on fire?"

"Give me your key," he said to her and turned to the policeman. "Keep an eye on her, I'm going to get her dog."

"Which unit is on fire! Please!" Roxanne handed him her keys, with the apartment key in her index fingers. She watched him run inside, *Memphis Fire* in reflective lettering on the back of his coat. "Her name is Lyla," she screamed out to him.

He disappeared into the stairwell.

CHAPTER SIX

"Miss, we need you to stand across the street with the others. I'm sure your dog's okay," the policeman said.

"You don't know that," Roxanne said, with her feet planted. "You don't know that at all." Her arm raised, she caressed her locket between her left index finger and thumb.

"We got word the fire's almost out. It was contained to a storage unit with faulty wiring. Let's wait across the street with the others. They'll let you inside soon." He put his hand lightly on her upper back and with gentle pressure guided her to the crowd of neighbors. A news team had set up their gear at the curb. Firefighters, inline on a ladder which was affixed to their truck, snaked the hose up to the lead man as he sprayed the top of the building.

Roxanne's gaze was fixed to the front door. The minutes felt like hours until the front door opened and she saw Lyla's black furry head. The firefighter held her under his arm and was petting her as he strode to Roxanne.

Roxanne ran across the street to meet him and lifted her pup out of his arms. "You little rascal, you scared me to death! Are you okay, baby?" She kissed the top of her head, her black fur smelled of smoke.

Lyla's feathered tail wagged as she licked her owner's face.

"She's okay," the firefighter said. "All the apartments on your end are. It was the other end of the hall that got hit." He took off his hat and wiped the sweat from his reddened forehead. "She's probably fine but I don't know how much smoke she took in. You might wanna have a vet check her out."

"I'll take her right now." She read his name in reflective block letters on the front of the fire jacket. "Lieutenant Gray, I'm going to bake you the best brownies you've *ever* eaten."

"That's not necessary, hon," he said, turning back toward the truck. "Just doing my job."

She carried Lyla to her double-parked car and drove a mile down the street to the Emergency Vet Clinic. She grabbed a leash from the trunk. "Let's go, baby." The sun had set but the streetlights gave plenty of illumination. She signed in, found a seat next to a bulldog and his human look-alike, and pulled out her smartphone. While she searched "smoke inhalation and dogs," she noticed a missed call. She didn't recognize the number so she listened to the voice message on speaker, her index finger hovered over the delete icon.

"Hey, Rox."

Justin.

She took it off speaker and held the phone to her ear.

"Wanted you to know, when I rounded on Anthony, he asked me to thank you. You leave a lasting impression on all the men in your path, I guess. Give me a call when you get this if you don't mind. Wanted to run something by you."

"What in the world's Justin calling about? Huh?" she said to Lyla. "Should I call him back, baby?"

Roxanne returned the call.

"Hello?" A youthful female voice said.

"Um, is Justin there?"

"One sec." Roxanne could hear her set the phone down and holler out, "Your phone."

Roxanne wanted to hang up. She could hear some muffled noise in the distance, a dog barked, and then his voice. "Hello?"

"It's Roxanne, you called?"

While your girlfriend was making your damn dinner.

"Hey!" he said. "What's going on?"

"Let's see…my dog was rescued from a burning building."

"Dude! Everything okay?"

"I'm waiting for the vet to check her out, but she looks okay." She cleared her throat. "I didn't know you had my cell."

"I hope you don't mind, I asked Keith to find it at the boardrunner's desk. My kid sister Megan's having a laparoscopy at the end of next month to check for endometriosis and I was wondering if you would do her anesthesia."

"Of course, I'd be honored to."

"That was her, who answered the phone. She's living with me while she's in med school. She's nervous about anesthesia…never had surgery. Would you mind talking to her?"

"Sure," Roxanne said.

"Thanks, I'll get her… hey, I really appreciate it."

After she spoke with his sister and reassured her, she ended the call and shook her head. For a brief moment she allowed herself to picture her life with a man in it again. Not just a stupid, careless, one-night stand. Justin was someone tangible, someone real. He was smart and sexy and kind. Like Mark had been. But he was also someone she could love and lose…like Mark.

No. I am not going down that road again.

She was going to take care of his sister and that was it. No need to get all worked up about it, she thought. Lyla was okay and that was all the love she needed right now.

CHAPTER SEVEN

While Roxanne and D.K. had been on a rooftop watching the Harahan Bridge light display, Geeta and Suvir De Silva were walking the bridge. Geeta stepped on fresh sawdust on the metal pedestrian path that had opened that day and laughed at a lab puppy that refused to walk on the reflective floor beneath him. The puppy whimpered and pulled against his leash, lying down in a last attempt of defiance. His owner, a heavily bearded twenty-something in jeans, picked him up and draped him on his shoulders. The dog looked pleased as he rested his muzzle on top of his owner's Memphis Red Birds baseball cap.

The sun was setting; the sky was orange with reflected pink clouds. "The bridge should light up any minute. Remember when the M lit for the first time?" Suvir said, pointing north to the iconic Hernando de Soto Bridge across from them.

"Honey, that was thirty years ago. I was pregnant with Anjali," Geeta said. "We're getting so old."

"We aren't old."

She pointed to her temples. Her long black straight hair had just recently begun to show gray. "Okay, *I'm* getting old. It's time to start coloring my hair."

"Don't you dare. I love your natural hair. And since when did you want to ingest all those chemicals?" He kissed the heart-shaped birthmark above her right eye.

It was good to be loved, she thought. If he didn't mind her gray, then why should she? And, anyway, grandmothers could have gray hair. Anjali, their only child, was expecting her first baby. As they walked, the fireworks began across the Mississippi River in West Memphis, and the sky filled with sparks. Suvir pulled Geeta to the side and held her close from behind. The metal pillars of their bridge lit in pink and green and yellow, almost as bright as the fireworks.

"I love that one. Looks like someone threw handfuls of glitter into the sky," Geeta said, her chin tilted toward the night sky. She felt Suvir squeeze her waist and she turned her head to kiss him.

She felt the metal flooring vibrate underneath her as two teenage boys skateboarded toward them. That wasn't a good idea with the bridge being so crowded, she thought. She stepped to scoot her and Suvir out of the way just as one of the kid's skateboards rolled over a loose screw. The front wheels skidded, causing the kid to careen forward, and he landed with his substantial weight onto Geeta. Suvir attempted to hold her, but she hit the ground firmly on her tailbone, while her neck whipped backward. "Mother Mary, Joseph!" she cried.

"I'm so sorry ma'am, I'm sorry." The kid got up and brushed the sawdust off his hands, extending his arm to help her. "I don't know what happened. Are you okay?" His friend skated back toward them.

"Let's get you up honey, grab my arm," Suvir said, as he lifted under her shoulders. "It's okay, kids. I've got her."

Her right lumbar region throbbed and she felt she couldn't stand straight. Her neck ached too.

"Oh it hurts," she whispered not wanting to further upset the teenager. "It's okay, dear, it was an accident. I'm fine."

Once the kids skated away she said, "I wish we could skate off this bridge too." She rubbed the back of her neck and looked along the path they had taken. "The parking lot looks miles away."

In the darkened sky, the firework show was at its finale. As the colors exploded above them Suvir bent at his waist and patted himself. "Piggyback?"

They were quite the pair, she thought, as she straddled his back and he lifted her. They were a middle-aged couple acting as they had back at a Christian camp four decades ago.

"It's better for me you're always dieting." He laughed and caressed her arm, which she'd draped over his shoulders. "Remember the color wars we used to play at camp?"

"I was just thinking that!" She hugged him and kissed the back of his neck. She'd take some Advil and a hot bath with Epsom salts, she thought, certain she'd feel better in the morning. She had a baby shower to prepare for next month. There was no time for this nonsense.

Geeta had originally disagreed when she'd heard the date for Anjali's shower that morning. She and Anjali were baking oatmeal cookies for the church fundraiser, when Anjali insisted the baby shower happen the third week of November.

"It'll be the holiday season soon and no one will show" Anjali said. "You know how many gatherings everyone has, with family and work parties."

"So have it in January," Geeta said. "It's bad luck to have it too soon."

"I'm not going to want the party when I'm about to go into labor," Anjali said, rubbing her baby bump. "And it's better to have gifts early and know what's left to buy." As Anjali bent to kiss her mom's forehead, Geeta inhaled her scent. Her daughter literally smelled of the sugar and spice from the cookie batter, and she found it hard to disagree with such an exquisite creature. Her baby.

"Don't be superstitious," Anjali said, and licked the frosting off her index finger. "Everything will be fine."

⌒

The day of the shower arrived. Geeta's twin sister, Rekha, hosted at her home across town. The ground was blanketed by red and yellow freshly fallen leaves, and Anjali's college friends and cousins were gathered. Geeta's contribution to the decorations was Anjali's thirty-year-old christening gown which hung with a pink bow on the front door. The aroma from the hors d'oeuvres table permeated the room, as did the laughter of the young women.

Geeta gave Anjali a hug. "You won, like you always do." As she stroked her daughter's thick black hair, Geeta tried not to grimace from pain. Her neck was getting worse; the fall on the bridge had caused some injury but she refused to attend to it.

"You two, freeze." Rekha said, from across the dining table with her Canon lens pointed on them. "Oh, that's a great shot," she said, reviewing the picture. "Baby G. Why are you doing that?"

"Doing what?" Geeta said. Only her twin called her Baby G.

"You're turning your head funny," Rekha said. "Why?"

"I fell, my neck's sore is all. Let's get everyone into the other room."

The flock of women was herded into the living room, where pink roses adorned the coffee table. Anjali, seated in an oversized armchair, began to unwrap presents while the twins stood at the entrance observing.

"Hard to believe she's all grown," Geeta said, watching as Anjali held up a floral baby romper against her belly.

"Yeah, and we didn't age a day," Rekha bit into a mini sandwich. "At least *I* didn't."

"Every inch of you looks like me," Geeta winced again and massaged her left shoulder.

"Seriously, your neck."

"It's fine."

"Go see my physical therapist," Rekha pulled her phone from her back pocket and scrolled through her contacts. "He's the best. I just sent you his details. Go."

"I will. Now, come on, let's enjoy our baby's baby celebration."

As Geeta watched her daughter, her upper back felt as though a knife was being thrust into her repeatedly. She excused herself to the kitchen and rummaged in her purse for the bottle of Percocet her internist had ordered. After downing two tablets, she found a seat in the living room. No amount of discomfort would keep her away from this.

CHAPTER EIGHT

Roxanne suffered insomnia before Megan Kirkland's surgery. Taking care of a physician was taxing, but Megan was a medical student *and* Justin's sister, intensifying Roxanne's unease. She tried to ignore the superstition among health care workers that bad things happen to nurses and doctors as patients, but her rapid heart rate last night refused to cooperate with reason.

She arrived to pre-op with her hair down, and a little mascara and lip gloss applied. The anesthesia tech, Keith, gave an approving look as she passed. She hoped Justin would too. She grabbed some alcohol swabs from the anesthesia cart and wiped the bell of her stethoscope. It was a ritual she'd repeated thousands of times, before and after each patient she examined.

She found Kirkland written on the dry erase board, with slot number three next to it. A petite brunette, whose only resemblance to Justin were her piercing green eyes, lay on a stretcher watching as Roxanne strode to her.

"I'm Roxanne, you're Megan?"

"If I have to be." Megan's voice had a faint tremble to it. Roxanne understood. She had been a complete hypochondriac her first year in medical school, every new disease she'd read about was somehow happening to her or her family. She was convinced a mole on Mark was melanoma and dragged him to their dermatology professor's office hours only to be told it was a freckle. She understood now worrying was useless. It was the things you never worried about that turned your world upside down.

"It's natural to be a little nervous. I'll give you the 'I don't care' drugs," Roxanne said. "That'll make everything so much easier. But first, can you sit

27

up?" Roxanne placed her stethoscope on Megan and then checked her lab work in the chart; the pregnancy test was negative.

"You've been having pelvic pain?"

"Incapacitating cycles. I've missed lectures because my cramps are so painful." She moved her bangs out of her eyes.

"Sounds difficult, I'm certain Dr. Huntington will find a benign explanation for it all. It's usually endometriosis, as you know. So, let me place the IV..." Roxanne wiped Megan's hand with an alcohol wipe and placed a tourniquet around her arm. "Justin's working today?"

Megan didn't flinch with the needle. "He has clinic this morning, but he'll be here later. Our mom's in the waiting room. I didn't want her back here. She's more nervous than me."

"Okay, all set, and you're going to do great." Roxanne taped down the IV site and noticed Dr. Heather Huntington at the doorway. Dr. Huntington, whose wild curly blond hair was already pulled into a cap, waved to her. "And here comes Liz, she's the OR nurse with us."

Liz wore only three earrings today. As she and Roxanne rolled the stretcher to the OR, Roxanne injected midazolam into Megan's IV. It took effect.

"Roxanne," Megan mumbled, "My brother's got a huge crush on you."

Midazolam not only relieved anxiety, but it was also referred to as truth serum. Roxanne had listened to many confessions from patients after they received it, the most memorable from a local church minister declaring she looked like his mistress. It's totally inappropriate to ask Megan any details, Roxanne thought.

Liz and Roxanne got Megan positioned on the OR table, placed the intra-operative monitors on her, and gave her oxygen by the face mask.

"You're doing fantastic," Roxanne said.

Megan replied, but her words were incoherent as she drifted off.

"Well now, that was interesting, huh? Quite the confession?"

"Liz, she was drugged, a totally unreliable witness," Roxanne said.

"She seemed coherent enough to me," Liz said. "And I've watched that man flirt with you."

"Who flirts?" Dr. Huntington said. She was positioning Megan's legs in stirrups. "What did I miss?"

"Nothing, you missed nothing," Roxanne said, with a look of pleading to Liz. "What do you think's wrong with this girl, Heather?"

The procedure was smooth and completed in under an hour. When the incisions were closed, Roxanne turned off the anesthesia gas. Megan opened her eyes. They moved Megan off the operating table and onto a stretcher, and took her down the hall to recovery.

Nick stood in the middle of the room and waved them over to him. His arms were up and bent, like signaling a plane into a hangar. A month had passed since Roxanne had slept with him, and she regretted it more with each passing day.

"Nick, how're you?" she said, turning her back to him as she put the EKG leads on Megan. "So this patient's healthy, no allergies, straightforward laparoscopy," she said. "Also she's Justin Kirkland's kid sister. Still pretty groggy, was a really cheap date, barely got any pain meds." When she turned again to face Nick, she saw Justin.

"How about you?" Justin said. "You a cheap date?" He wore slacks and a buttoned-down shirt; his white lab coat had a resident badge on the sleeve. He stood with his hand on the foot of his sister's stretcher. Roxanne took off her blue bouffant cap, letting her long curls fall loosely by her face. She glanced quickly at Nick and felt as though she was on stage; a bright light solo performance and he was in the front row.

Roxanne didn't think there was anything cheap about herself, yet without question she'd been a cheap date for Nick. "Megan did great," she said.

"I knew you'd make sure of it," Justin said. "Did Huntington find anything?"

"She'll update you once Megan's awake," Roxanne said. "But nothing to worry about, a dermoid cyst."

"Thanks, again." Justin ran his fingers through his widow's peak. The silver streak caught her eye.

"She seems like a great kid sister; you don't look alike though."

Except for those bedroom eyes.

"I was going...to ask you," he said, as he watched his sister sleep.

Roxanne's smartphone rang. She looked at the display; it was her partner Alfonzo, probably with her next assignment. She turned her phone to mute.

"May I take you to dinner?" Justin said. "As thanks?"

Roxanne glanced at Nick. His expression one of a champion poker player, she thought.

"That would be nice," she said. "I'll talk to you later. I have to go answer this call."

He smiled at Roxanne, pulled a chair next to his sister's stretcher and sat. Nick pushed a button on the monitor and the blood pressure cuff cycled, then he reached over and took Megan's oxygen mask off her face.

Roxanne walked out of recovery to find Alfonzo.

Nick, please don't tell Justin!

She heard Alfonzo before she saw him. His shoes were squeaking on the linoleum as he walked down the corridor.

"What's up Rothanasia?" Dr. Alfonzo Weddington said. If Alfonzo considered you a friend, he'd have a nickname or two for you. Dr. Roxanne Roth had several; Ro-Ro, Roxy, She-Rox.

With deep brown eyes and dimples, Alfonzo arrived to work every day wearing gray scrubs and bright blemish-free sneakers—in an array of colors depending on his mood. Today they were magenta.

His organizational skills lent him to be "board runner" most days; a position in which he arranged the operating schedule for the entire anesthesia department. He was an attentive, compassionate doctor but also valued his life out of the hospital. He drove the latest Mercedes-Benz convertible; "Always lease 'em, Roxy." Come fall, he went to the basement with "the fellas" with a Cohiba cigar clamped in his lips and his family knew not to disturb them for the next three hours of Sunday football. He and the fellas once crashed a private party hosted by a golf legend. The night ended with them swimming in their boxer shorts in the host's pool. And though he liked his time with the guys, he adored his wife. At the department's annual holiday party, the two could be cover models from *Essence* magazine. "One house, one spouse," he preached to any partner who would listen.

"Missed your call," Roxanne said as she put her hair back into a cap.

They walked to the main operating room control desk and Alfonzo studied the dry erase board where cases were handwritten in block letters. "Webb's got a single level neck fusion uncovered. You know him? New guy from Los Angeles."

"Not new to me, and not from LA. Local boy. I went to medical school with him." Roxanne draped her stethoscope around her neck.

"He any good?"

"No idea. We never had any clinicals together. He was one of the top of our class though. Competitive. Aggressive, actually."

"I heard about his case from a few weeks back that didn't go well. The lady woke up paraplegic. Med exec's reviewing it."

"But they're letting him operate?"

"No matter how well they trained him, he no longer has staff looking over his shoulder to help out. Let's hope it was a fluke."

She saw the case written on the whiteboard. ACDF. Room 20. Anterior cervical disc fusion, she thought. He would be making a small incision in the patient's neck, taking out injured tissue and stabilizing her neck with hardware. Every neurosurgeon she'd ever met was trained extensively in the procedure.

"I'll go set up," Roxanne said and headed down the hall. In the operating room she checked the anesthesia machine and noticed the backup oxygen tank was low. She texted Keith to replace it. She drew up her medications and locked them in the anesthesia cart. 4-2-5-1. Not exactly maximum security, but better than sitting out in the open.

She needed to evaluate her patient, but first she texted Claire.

Justin asked me out.

. . .

That. Is. Awesome.

. . .

Feeling anxious about it.

. . .

Make an appointment with your therapist. ASAP. Must discuss with her too.

Roxanne touched her necklace. She wanted to be happy. She wanted to be excited. But instead she mostly felt anxious.

...

<u>Okay. Will.</u>

She put her phone in the back pocket of her scrubs and walked the hallway to pre-op. It would be good to shift her focus back to a patient. She'd call her therapist later.

CHAPTER NINE

D.K. rode the vacant staff elevator to the fifth floor and buttoned the top of his white lab coat with its freshly embroidered logo above the breast pocket. *MEMPHIS NEUROSURGICAL.* His solo private practice was promoted with a slick commercial featuring himself and a mature actress locals recognized as a hometown girl who succeeded in Hollywood. "Minimally invasive spine surgery by the best for the best, serving our great city of Memphis," the former starlet said into the camera. He'd been aggressive in recruiting referrals, visiting neurology and physical therapy clinics with stacks of business cards. Unlike most of his competitors, he accepted Medicare and the region desperately needed another spine specialist, so his clinic quickly booked up.

Wiping perspiration from his forehead, he walked into pre-op and read the dry erase board. WEBB. Slot 9. He spotted his patient, Mrs. Welty, lying on a stretcher. With her obese neck, it wasn't going to be easy to find the disc. As he approached, he saw Roxanne by the stretcher. His day was getting even better. After the morning spent enjoying Crystal's body, he could now work with and on Roxanne. She'd be great to have on rotation.

"Long time no see, classmate," he said, close enough that he could smell her shampoo. It reminded him of apples and roses. "You doing my case?"

"Welcome back, I figured we'd eventually work together." She stepped away from him and faced the computer workstation. "We've been ready for over an hour."

You work for me, he thought. I brought the patient here, not you.

"No foley," he said.

"I'm not responsible for putting in urinary catheters, D.K."

"Yeah, I just mean tell the nurse when you see her." He took out a surgical marking pen from his lab coat pocket and spoke to his patient. "Which side hurts you again, dear?"

Mrs. Welty had a moon-shaped face and stubby hands. "It's on the right, down to my hand," she said, moving her right fingers.

"Can you sit up?" he said. Her flesh spilled out of her hospital gown. He scribbled D.K.W. on the right side of her neck. "I'll see you in the OR. Which room are we in, Roxanne?" He put the marker back in his breast pocket.

"OR twenty."

He went to change clothes. The smell of bloodied scrubs wafted from the linen basket as he walked into the men's locker room. He opened his locker and took a swig of vodka from the thermos he kept before changing into clean scrubs. This would be fun, he thought, changing his mind about the quick clean case he'd planned. He tied the drawstrings against his flat abdomen, the result of decades of tennis.

⌒

Roxanne's patient was intubated, the sterile drapes clipped to IV poles on either side of the patient as D.K. worked on Mrs. Welty's neck. The patient's heart rate had been steadily increasing as her blood loss continued. Roxanne looked over the blue drape and watched as D.K., motionless, stared into the surgical field as it filled with blood. The surgical tech next to him offered up a gauze.

"D.K, should we call vascular for back up?" She hung a unit of blood on the IV pole, the patient's second. "I'm going to have to start pressors soon if you don't get it under control."

"There's no need to call anyone. I got it."

Roxanne reached for a syringe of epinephrine. She held it above the drape at eye level to show him.

"Don't make me push epi on an ACDF."

He continued to watch the blood pool at the site. "I need some thrombin." The surgical tech handed him a small white square soaked in clotting factors to help stop the bleed. He sutured, at a medical student's pace, in no rush to stop the bloodletting.

Roxanne raised her voice. "We need a foley. I've given her over six liters of fluid and blood." She realized her order would be a challenge to fill since the patient was under sterile blue drapes, but she needed the bladder emptied or it could rupture from being distended.

"I said no foley," D.K. said.

"Why don't you stop the bleed and stop telling me how to manage my patient." Roxanne waved to the nurse to continue as she and another nurse lifted the blue drapes to work underneath, careful not to break the sterile boundary. A few minutes later, a plastic bag connected to a long plastic tube filled with a liter of yellow fluid.

When D.K. closed the wound three hours later, a liter of blood had been lost. The suction canisters were full. "Not my fault her neck belongs on a walrus, not a woman," D.K. said, glancing at the canisters. He went to the head of the bed and took off his sterile gloves and gown. "Roxanne, why haven't you extubated yet?"

"Do you not see how swollen she is? I ordered an ICU bed two hours ago. I'm not extubating her today."

"Whatever, do it your way, scaredy girl, but she's fine. I told you I could fix it," he said.

He walked out.

Exasperated, Roxanne and the team transferred the patient to the ICU. She spoke with the nurse, assisted the respiratory therapist with the breathing tube, and asked the unit secretary to page the resident on call for the night.

"Looks like you've been busy," Justin said. He'd changed into scrubs and was drinking a soda. "Is this what you got called away to do?"

"And it was no fun. How's Megan?"

"She's good, no nausea, sleeping at our parents' home tonight since I'm on call here."

"So this is Webb's ACDF. Welty's her name." She and Justin examined her. "Her face's a little swollen as you can see but her vitals and labs are okay. She moves all extremities when I wake her."

"What happened? Wasn't it a single-level disc?"

35

Roxanne lowered her voice. "Webb sliced the right vertebral artery."

"Damn."

"I gave her four units of blood and she's probably got sleep apnea, too. I didn't want to extubate her until the swelling resolved."

Roxanne motioned for Justin to follow her into the hall away from the nurses. She whispered to him, "Webb was sweating the entire time, even in pre-op. He fidgeted the whole case."

"Sounds like the meth head I just admitted."

"You know, actually, he was like a meth head. I'm going to get this reviewed by the med exec committee, so be meticulous with documentation."

"For sure I will." Justin bent his head closer. "So, when may I please have dinner with you?"

Roxanne felt her shoulders relax for the first time that day. "I'm off for the holiday. You?"

He opened the calendar on his smartphone.

"On call Thanksgiving and Sunday, how about Friday?"

"Friday's good," she said.

"I'll pick you up at eight? Text me the address."

Roxanne picked up her clipboard and paperwork from the counter. "Will do." She turned the corner and glanced at the chipped pink polish on her fingernails. She'd been planning on going straight to the library to study for the boards but decided it could wait. She needed a manicure, and some wine.

CHAPTER TEN

When Friday arrived, she took a seemingly endless shower, letting the warm water cascade onto her as she meditated. After three outfit changes and spending an hour on her hair and makeup, she examined herself in the full-length mirror. Her blue eyes with black mascara looked larger with contacts instead of eyeglasses. She felt physically, if not emotionally, ready for Justin. Then at eight o'clock she panicked. *These black jeans are too tight. Why did I buy another pair of tight jeans?* She debated changing. Again.

The doorbell rang. It was too late.

She cracked the door open, peeked, and opened the door. It was the first time she'd seen him clean-shaven and out of scrubs. He had on a midnight blue button-down shirt, untucked and completely unbuttoned, with a fitted white T-shirt underneath. She could make out the silhouette of his muscular torso. His jeans were as loose as his smile. There were no blood or drapes between them tonight, just clear skin and healthy hormones. His gaze took her in.

Lyla jumped at him, standing on her back paws as if inviting him to tango.

"Off Lyla!"

"It's okay, I don't mind. I've got a beagle mutt at home." Justin squatted and pet Lyla. "Do you smell my dog on me, Lyla, is that it?" The dog was beside herself, trying to lick his face off.

"What breed is she?" Justin turned to Roxanne while still kneeling and petting Lyla.

"Some spaniel mix? She's a rescued stray."

"You look great," he said, standing.

"Yeah, you do too." She gave him an inviting hug and breathed in his smell, faint and musky. Manly. "Can I get you a drink?"

"Sure, whatever you're having." When they walked into the living room he whistled. "Killer place. I should've matched into anesthesia. Is that a deck?"

Roxanne poured a Joseph Phelps cabernet into two wine glasses. She handed one to Justin as Lyla continued to paw his leg for attention. "She likes you. She's usually skittish around men she doesn't know unless they're rescuing her from a burning building."

"I sometimes have that effect on girls." He smiled that grin and sipped the wine, his gaze glued on her as they stood in her kitchen.

"Want to sit outside?" she said, tucking a strand of hair behind her ear.

They sat at the patio table on her wrap balcony, overlooking the Mississippi River to the west and part of downtown Memphis to the northeast. The sun had faded and the Hernando de Soto Bridge lit up in the familiar M formation. The Harahan Bridge was lit for the holiday in orange and brown.

"So one question. You're single, right?" Justin said.

"No, my husband's away this weekend." She reached across and poured him more wine. "Of course I'm single, Justin."

"Well, I've wanted to ask you out for a while, but I overheard you and Liz talking about a guy. Mark?"

Roxanne sipped her wine. She tucked the locket of her necklace under her blouse.

"That was when I was in medical school. Liz knew him."

"Okay." He reached over and put his hand over hers. She pulled it away.

"I don't want to talk about him, okay?" She stood and walked to the rail. She forced a smile back on her face before she faced him.

"Sure." He sipped the last of his wine, and set the glass down on the patio table. "Well, I'm glad I ignored Nick's advice." He leaned back in his chair.

Roxanne's heart dropped to her knees.

"Nick? Nurse Nick? From Recovery?"

"He tried to convince me that an anesthesiologist would never want to date a surgeon, because I'm the enemy."

"That's silly, I happen to like most surgeons I know. Not Webb, but most." She took both empty glasses inside and set them in the sink. "So you ready to head out?"

"If we have to." He looked at the couch. "It's so…inviting here."

"Yes. We have to!" She'd dealt with men treating her like a sex object her entire adult life, despite the MD behind her name. She wasn't about to have Justin disrespect her in her own home. "Exactly what else did Nick tell you?"

"Just that I was lucky."

He opened the front door for her and with a slight bow said, "After you, Dr. Roth."

They waited for the Riverfront loop trolley. The typical mix of tourists and downtown locals greeted them with curious glances as they waited to board the streetcar. She saw a blonde woman in baggy sweatpants take pictures of her condominium using a point-and-shoot camera.

"You're such a baller, that lady's impressed with your crib," Justin said.

Roxanne smiled at the lady in the trolley. "Shhh! Don't embarrass her."

The wine had them both giggling. She stumbled on the stairs of the trolley car and he caught her by the waist. "Good thing you're not driving, lightweight," he said into her ear and, holding her elbow, he guided her to one of the narrow wooden benches in the back of the trolley car. He sat next to her with his arm extended behind her on the wooden bench. His blue sleeve brushed her shoulder.

As the trolley rolled along South Main Street, they passed the Arcade Diner and art galleries. The old brick buildings were juxtaposed against new commercial space. The American Apparel had a billboard-sized poster hanging in the window of a barely teenage model in her bra and leggings.

"I made reservations at that sushi place on South Main, since you mentioned you enjoyed sushi in Brooklyn," he said. "We could go somewhere else, though."

"Sounds good." Maybe he hadn't meant any disrespect earlier, she thought.

A few blocks later the trolley was at their stop. "Peabody Place," hollered the female conductor. "Next stop, Union."

Justin stepped off the trolley and offered his hand to Roxanne. She took it and they continued to hold hands as they walked toward the restaurant, along Main Street's cobblestones. The night enveloped them like a warm hug. A breeze scattered the fallen maple tree leaves, and with nearly every step, a dry leaf crackled beneath them.

"Thanks for making the reservation, Justin. All of downtown is full on Grizzlies nights."

As they entered the restaurant, the techno music would not be denied. Two women in short skirts viewed Justin from the bar, while a group of four businessmen huddled near a flat-screen TV. The men watched the Grizzlies basketball game as well as Roxanne. The ceiling's blue track lighting illuminated them as the hostess led them to the back corner of the restaurant. Wall mirrors reflected them and Roxanne caught her reflection. She stood straighter. They were seated at a blue chaise sofa with a coffee table to dine on. A disco ball hung above their heads.

"Enjoy your meal," the hostess said, smiling, as she clicked away on her heels.

Justin sat next to Roxanne, leaned in, and spoke into her ear. "I didn't realize it's so loud in here." He glanced around, the place was at capacity.

"I like the vibe."

He opened his menu and she leaned in and read with him.

"What looks good to you?" he said.

"How about the combination plate, so we can sample a bit of everything?"

The waitress approached, her red hair pulled back into a loose bun, her eyes lingered on Justin. "How're y'all tonight? What can I get you to drink?"

"Want to split another bottle, Rox?"

She nodded.

"We'll have a bottle of the Joseph Phelps, and we'll share combination number five."

Justin handed her back the menu.

"Good choice." The redhead smiled at Justin. "I'll be right back with the wine." She walked away. Her skin-tight pants accentuated her figure and

Roxanne noticed that Justin's gaze followed the waitress as well. Shit, she thought. I'm competing with twenty-something redheads.

Justin stretched out and pulled a seat cushion beside his head. Patting the spot next to him, he motioned for her to recline with him on the chaise. Roxanne positioned herself on her elbow, with her legs crossed, facing Justin. She was glad she wore pants.

"So, it's just you and your sister? No brothers?"

"Nope, just us. I always wanted a brother though. Megan never wanted to play football with me. And you?"

"Just sis and I. We're pretty close. I talk to her every day." She pulled out her smartphone, and she leaned toward him. "This was from the Botanic Garden this spring." His hand covered hers to bring the phone, and her, closer. He studied the photo of Roxanne and Claire in front of cherry blossoms, Claire's arm slung over her sister.

"Y'all could be twins. Is she in medicine?"

"Social worker at the VA. She helps homeless vets and she's a saint. She's been my anchor to Memphis. Brooklyn was great, but living far away from her and my parents was lonely." She twirled a loose curl.

"I was homesick when I was at Northwestern. That's why I got Wrigley."

"Wrigley?"

"A beagle stray that hung around a Lincoln Park Café. I'd have coffee there most mornings. He always came up to me and sat on my feet like he owned me. After a few weeks I gave in and took him home." He drank a sip of the water. "I can't believe they actually won the World Series."

Roxanne had been too emotional to watch the series, knowing how happy Mark would've been. He'd been a Cubs fan since childhood after his father had taken him to his first game. She kept the ball he'd caught at Wrigley Field in her nightstand, next to his phone.

The wine arrived, forcing them to sit.

"To getting to know each other," Justin said. They clinked glasses.

"It's weird we both went to White Station but never met," she said.

"Well, you would've been a senior when I was but a wimpy freshman. You never would've noticed me."

"Never remind a woman that she's older than you, surgeon."

She looked over Justin's shoulders, feeling someone was looking at her. It was Webb. He was staring at her from the bar. He was with a gorgeous woman in a transparent thong leotard with half of her bottom exposed, her red pants slung low. She could see the woman's nipple piercing.

"Don't look, but Webb's here and he's staring at us."

Justin glanced behind him.

"He's staring at *you*. Looks like an interesting date he's got." Justin pushed the blue pillow back and turned toward her. His left leg was almost touching hers. "I don't blame him for looking at you."

"Do you know how Mrs. Welty did? His neck that bled on Monday?"

"I didn't want to tell you tonight, but she had a stroke. She's hoarse and having difficulty swallowing."

"D.K. refused vascular assist." Roxanne shook her head. "Do you know how frustrating it is to be completely helpless while watching a surgeon struggle?"

Justin reached over, his thumb brushed her lower cheek.

"You're far from helpless, she could've died without you."

Their dinner arrived, a spread of sushi as colorful as the coral reefs she and Mark had snorkeled above in Hawaii—the day after he'd asked her to get married.

As she sucked one end of an edamame, the other end popped open and a bean landed in Justin's lap.

"Oh my god I'm such a dork."

Justin's lopsided grin returned as he picked up the bean and placed it on the table. "There's a lot of food, huh?" He proceeded to eat most of the meal, admonishing her for not eating more. When the waitress removed their platter, Roxanne excused herself to the restroom. She stood looking at herself in the dimly lit bathroom mirror and reapplied her pink lip-gloss.

It's okay to like him.

She returned to their table to see the redhead give the leather check presenter to Justin. His credit card was sticking out of the top of it. He smiled at Roxanne and stood as she approached. He put his credit card in his wallet and returned the wallet to the back pocket of his jeans. "Ready to head out? Do you feel like walking?"

"Sure, I miss city walking."

Justin reached for her hand as they walked out of the restaurant, and they continued to hold hands as they strolled along the Mississippi Riverwalk. The river was cloaked in darkness but the bridge lights reflected onto it. The smell of a wood fire from a nearby home permeated the crisp air. Fall had arrived.

"How're your studies going for boards?" she said.

"Okay, I guess. I'll take a review course for the written test. I'm not ready for the oral boards at all."

"I passed the written anesthesiology board exam a few months ago and in the spring I have to take my orals," Roxanne said. His hand was large and strong, she liked the feel of it.

"I didn't know you guys have oral boards too."

"Two firing squads. Two cases. And I have to pass it to become a partner in my group too."

"Just like the surgical boards," he said. "Doing surgery and talking about it are completely different beasts."

"Can you believe they used to have us going in and out of hotel rooms to answer board exams? At least now we all go to North Carolina. To an actual testing center."

"They're sadists, I'm telling you."

"I'm dreading the call that it's scheduled then I really have to focus. If I don't pass I'll have to take time off until I do."

"We can study together at least. I'll be happy to give you mock oral exams." He squeezed her hand. "In a hotel room."

"Is that so?" She took her hand out of his and hooked it around his elbow, her hand on his bicep. He placed his other hand over hers. When they arrived at her doorstep, Roxanne's jitters began. She placed the keys in the lock and turned to face him.

"Thank you for dinner."

"Bring it in." He opened his arms.

Roxanne smiled, her eyes down, and entered his embrace. He held her tightly then pulled away a few inches. He raised her chin to look her in the eyes. "Great to see you outside of the hospital," he whispered.

He kissed her gently at first. His lips were soft and she could taste the wine. He smelled so good. She wrapped her arms around his neck and pulled him closer. His body leaned against hers.

Mark.

The wave of emotion hit her hard, like a sucker punch to her heart. Their last kiss had been in pre-op holding. She stepped away from Justin's embrace, turned her head down and dabbed her eyes with the sleeve of her shirt.

"You okay?"

She turned away from him and unlocked her apartment door. She stepped inside and Lyla jumped on her. Justin leaned against the doorway. He bent and pet Lyla's head. "I'll see you soon." His voice soft. He gave her cheek a kiss and walked to the elevator. She watched him as he put his arm against the back railing of the elevator and looked down. He disappeared behind the silver barriers as the elevator doors closed.

She shut her door and rested against it from inside her apartment.

CHAPTER ELEVEN

D.K. wasn't concerned that Mrs. Welty, his grossly obese patient, was unable to swallow. His surgery had cured her disc and he'd functionally given her a gastric bypass for free. She would lose all that weight, so she and her husband should be thanking him. The med exec board had already flagged the lumbar fusion from last month that woke paraplegic. Now they'd flagged Welty as well and he'd been "invited" to a review next week.

He sauntered into the sushi restaurant and found Crystal, as instructed, waiting for him at the bar. Her outfit was to his specifications as well. A white see-through leotard with the thong clearly visible on her perfect booty; her red skin-tight pants hung low. She wore a white choker further accentuating her perfect deep ebony complexion. Her nails and eyelashes were as long as they were fake. Costume jewelry bracelets decorated her wrists.

He caressed her pierced left nipple and kissed her neck. She smiled and kissed his cheek.

"Hey sexy," she said.

"Hi, my queen. You look like a tricked-out Halle Berry. I like it." He looked around the restaurant. "I like this place too."

The music was loud and the blue track lighting kept his face concealed, no need for shades to cover his dilated pupils. He surveyed the diners and his gaze quickly zoomed in on Roxanne across the room. She was lying on a chaise lounge sipping wine with some dude that looked familiar. Did that guy work in the hospital? He wasn't the same loser he saw her with at the rooftop party. She got around, he thought, and wondered when it would be his turn. He thought she'd seen him, but couldn't be sure.

His headache that morning had been rough. They'd become frequent during his college years playing tennis for the Ole Miss Rebels and had never gone away completely. But today's was different, more intense. He needed to lay off the coke for a bit. Or maybe the Molly he'd had the night before.

After downing two dirty martinis, he and Crystal walked toward Beale Street. The pedestrian road was crowded with Grizzlies fans walking to the game. He liked the reaction Crystal's outfit caused among them. Women whispered to each other and men elbowed one another to take a look. A group of University of Memphis fraternity boys followed them along the brick path of Beale Street. One of them said, "Hey dude, can I have her when you're done?" D.K. and Crystal looked behind them, and he grinned as she flipped them off. As they kept walking, his hand rested on her bottom.

They had to go through a metal detector to get into the FedEx Forum. He walked through it close to Crystal and when the alarm sounded, he ignored it and kept walking.

A security man sprinted after him.

"Sir, I'm going to need you to empty your pockets."

These rent-a-cops are a joke, thought D.K. He had an eight ball in his left front pocket which he'd been planning on snorting in the bathroom.

"Sure, man." D.K. pulled a Swiss Army knife from his right front pocket; a knife he'd stolen from a sporting goods store when he was seven. His first kill was a frog he'd found on his porch; he'd delighted in slicing open the frog's live belly, the insides still moving. It had been his favorite toy until he'd discovered his father's guns by age thirteen. His father trained him, and it didn't take long for him to become a sharpshooter, firing at targets outside his family's lake house in Greers Ferry, Arkansas.

"I forgot I had this on me," D.K. said with the folded knife in his palm.

"I'll have to confiscate it."

"No one touches my knives, man."

Crystal came close to the guard and hooked her arm around his. "Couldn't you just hold it instead, this one time?" She rubbed against him.

"Yeah. Yeah, I could hold it. For you." The guard stared at her breasts through the transparent leotard. "Come find me after the game, sweetheart."

"Or if you'd prefer, you could just let me hold onto it?" she said, her fingers touched in between her breasts. She smiled and leaned forward to give him the full view. "Please?"

The guard had never seen such an incredible body. His dad would've called her "a brick house." He stared at her breasts. "Just go ahead," he said, adjusting his crotch. "You're a lucky son of a bitch." He muttered to D.K.

"Yeah, I am." D.K. held her hand as they walked away. He leaned into her and said, "I didn't need your help. I was handling it." He tucked the knife back into his pocket. "You do what I tell you to do, remember that."

"Sugar, I just want you to have fun, is all." She kissed his cheek. "You wanna go bone in the family bathroom?"

"I'll tell you when we screw too." He took a generous squeeze of her bottom before slapping it. "Later."

They walked down the stairs to his season ticket floor seats. The game had already begun and the crowd erupted with cheers when Marc Gasol hit a three-pointer. A team photographer who was on the sidelines across from them zoomed his lens on Crystal. He snapped a few pictures before he turned the lens back onto the game.

D.K. flipped through the game's playbook and he found what he was looking for. MEMPHIS NEUROSURGICAL. Minimally invasive surgery by the best, for the best. Damn right, he thought. He was going to build an empire. Soon everyone in this arena would know who he was.

CHAPTER TWELVE

⌒

The sound of Lyla whimpering by her bed woke Roxanne. 0950. Her interpretation of time influenced by medical records always reflecting if it was morning or night. She patted her bed, inviting Lyla to hop on. While she pet her she reached into her nightstand where she kept Mark's phone. It was fully charged since she was terrified to lose their conversation thread, their digital diary. She scrolled through their texts from five years ago.

Did you find a deal on a new car? She'd written.

Still Looking! It has to be classy enough to carry you.

Is there such car?:)

Roxanne got out of bed, stretching the sleep out of her right shoulder as Lyla pawed at her legs. "Okay, okay. Walk. I got it."

Lyla bounded to the front door and stared at the doorknob. Roxanne's hair was wild, she thought, with a glance at the mirror. She pulled baggy sweatpants and a red PUMA T-shirt out of the dryer and slipped her bare feet into her sneakers. She grabbed her cell phone, keys, and the prescription sunglasses that lay on the foyer table. "Good girl, let's go." She hooked Lyla's leash to her collar.

Once they were out of the elevator with good cell coverage, she phoned Claire.

"How was the date?" Roxanne heard a train whistle through the phone.

"Come work out with me and I'll tell you. And maybe you can help me with a mock exam or two?"

48

"I'll just listen and nod, but sure." Claire laughed. "You always sound brilliant to me."

Her sister arrived after Roxanne had walked Lyla along the river.

"Aren't you looking fit," Roxanne said, embracing Claire. "Work out, then brunch?"

Claire, dressed in black spandex pants and a pink sports bra, unzipped her fleece jacket and hung it behind a kitchen barstool. Like Roxanne, she had the figure of a pin-up girl. Unlike Roxanne, her hair was straight. "You always want the hair you can't have," Claire had once said while playing with one of Roxanne's tendrils.

"I brought strawberries and..." Claire rummaged through the kitchen cabinets and pulled out a mix box and a bottle of maple syrup. "Let's put them on pancakes."

"Only after we log an hour on cardio," Roxanne said.

They began their workout in her condo's fitness center, side by side on the elliptical machines. Lyla lay on the floor in front of them, her head following the conversation, turning from one to the other, until she dozed off. The "No Dogs Allowed" sign hung behind her.

"So you're smitten?"

"More like terrified."

"Oh, hon, it's okay."

Roxanne used the remote control to switch the channel from news to a music video station. A pop star was singing in a leotard with a live snake draped over her shoulders. "I don't think I'm ready. I won't survive another heartache."

"No, you can't think like that." She increased the incline on her elliptical and reached across to increase Roxanne's as well. Roxanne groaned.

"What happened to Mark was a fluke. A tragedy. But it won't happen again."

"You can't promise that."

"It's time sis, to move forward. You haven't been with a man in five years."

Nick doesn't count, Roxanne thought. No one, even her sister, needed to know about her indiscretion.

"You should let Justin *in*." Claire reached for the remote and flipped the channels, settling back on the music channel.

"It's been one date."

"I'm just sayin'. Did you tell him about Mark?"

"Not yet."

They continued the rest of their workout watching music videos, both with increasingly labored breathing. After an hour of intense climbing, they stepped off the equipment. Claire dabbed her forehead with a sports towel while Roxanne stretched. Claire wiped down both machines with the antibacterial wipes dispensed by the water fountain. They walked back to the apartment as Lyla led.

"That got my glutes for sure. I feel it already," Claire said.

"Ditto." Roxanne unlocked her condo door and immediately searched for her smartphone.

Had a great time. Free again Friday night?

She bit her lower lip and texted back.

Bring Wrigley, play date for the pups? I'll cook.

A smile formed as she read his reply.

Sounds fun, see you at 7.

Roxanne noticed her sister's bemused smile. Claire pulled out a kitchen barstool and sat to peel an orange from the fruit bowl on the counter. "Justin, right? Looks like you're heading in the right direction." She handed her a piece of the orange.

As the taste of orange filled Roxanne's mouth she thought a silent prayer.

CHAPTER THIRTEEN

"It looks like Santa threw up in here," Suvir said, setting a heavy cardboard box in front of the Christmas tree.

"Is that the last of them?" Geeta glanced at the box and rubbed the heart-shaped birthmark above her right eye, a habit she'd had since childhood. She was on a step stool, hanging an angel made from white yarn and wire onto the tree. She and Anjali had made an ornament every year since Anjali was two years old.

"Yes, all fourteen boxes." Suvir took a deep breath in. "I love that smell. Fresh pine."

Geeta took his hand and stepped off the stool to admire their work. The tree was covered in silver tinsel, white lights, and colorful ornaments. Anjali would call it "nuclear." On the mantle were red and white embroidered stockings: *Suvir, Geeta, Anjali, Kohi*, and now a new small pink stocking. The baby's name wasn't embroidered on it yet; Anjali and Kohi hadn't decided on one.

"Remember when Anjali opened her first bike? Right there." She pointed to the left of the tree.

She looked inside the last box and picked up a snowman they'd bought at an estate sale. She felt a pop in her neck. White ceramic shattered on the hardwood floor.

"Honey!" She raised her hand to her neck.

"What happened?" he said, immediately at her side, his arm around her waist.

Geeta leaned forward to pick up the head of the snowman.

"Leave it, leave it. Come here." He guided her to the couch. "Please sit."

"I just couldn't hold onto it. I don't know what happened." She sat. "All of a sudden I felt a pop. My neck."

Suvir went to the kitchen cabinet and found the anti-inflammatory pills his doctor had prescribed for his kidney stone last month. He handed it to her with a glass of water. While she drank, he got a broom and swept the ceramic off the floor into a dustpan. "It's time you see a neurosurgeon. Your therapist isn't helping." He dumped the dustpan into the garbage can under the kitchen sink. "Where's that card he gave you?"

"In my wallet, in my purse." She pointed to her bag hanging off the kitchen cabinet door handle. "But PT *is* helping me. I don't need a surgeon."

"You're losing strength in that arm. You should do those nerve blocks he suggested." Suvir rummaged through her purse until he read the card. <u>Memphis Neurosurgical. By the best, for the best</u>.

"And no one will block you until a neurosurgeon orders it." He handed the card to her. "Let's just go see what he has to say?"

"It couldn't hurt." She noticed her pinky and ring finger were both tingling now. That was new. She held the glossy card with the raised font and extra thick paper. "D.K. Webb, MD. I'll call Monday morning," she said, looking at the baby stocking. "But I don't want any procedures until the baby's born, Anjali needs me."

"Anjali needs grandma to be well. That's what Anjali needs." Suvir kissed the top of her head and stroked her thick black ponytail. "And so do I."

CHAPTER FOURTEEN

With the lasagna in the oven, Roxanne's condo smelled like an Italian eatery. She found a YouTube channel on her Apple TV and played Italian dinner music. "To complete the mood," she said. Justin danced with the dogs at his feet at the song, "We no speak Americano."

"You look like Charlie Chaplin on crack," she said, taking a bite of the garlic bread she'd left to cool. "Dinner's almost ready." She sat on the couch and turned the music down. A woman was singing an Italian ballad. Lyla and Wrigley had befriended after a few sniffs. They hopped on either side of her. The long walk along the river had tired them out.

"Hey, do you know what McNugget is slang for?" Roxanne said.

Justin laughed at her question. "Someone called you a McNugget?" He took the cushioned seat next to Wrigley.

"Yeah, what does it mean?"

"First tell me who said it!"

"Some teenagers, just some kids hanging outside the liquor store down the street. I walked by them this afternoon to buy wine and I overheard one of them call me a McNugget." She petted Wrigley. "Does it mean brown on the outside?"

Justin laughed so hard she could see the back of his throat. "What is so funny!" He had an incredible laugh, she thought. It came from deep inside him and was contagious.

When Justin stopped laughing, he held both her hands. "McNugget's slang, doll. They said you were good enough. To eat."

"Oh." Roxanne blushed. "I thought it was some racial thing. Because I have like a permanent tan."

This threw Justin into hysterics again and he wiped his eyes with the sleeve of his red polo sweatshirt. "Well, I'd have to agree with those guys." He leaned forward and kissed her. "You're a total McNugget."

Roxanne withdrew mid-kiss.

"You okay?" He scooted away from her while keeping his arm on the couch cushion behind her. "Did I offend you?" Wrigley moved his head onto Justin's lap.

"No, it's fine. I just need a minute." Roxanne walked into her bedroom. The tears had formed, again. She sat on her bed for a few minutes and picked at her nails.

When Roxanne walked back into the living room, Justin had her oven mitt on and was taking the lasagna out of the oven. "Thought it looked ready," he said, setting it on the stovetop. "You want to eat?" He took the oven mitt off.

She checked the pan. "Let's give it some time to cool." She took his hand in hers. "There's something I need to tell you."

"Okay." He ran his other hand through his dark hair, the silver streak in the center more obvious now that his hair had grown out an inch.

"Come sit for a second." She led him outside to the deck, and sat in a chair next to him. The dogs followed them, sniffing and jumping. Roxanne looked north at the downtown skyline. She could see the FedEx Forum and AutoZone Park in the distance. It was cool enough outside that she needed a jacket over her blouse.

"I haven't talked with you about my fiancé, Mark. It was five years ago. That's what you overheard Liz and me speaking about. A lot of people in the hospital knew him."

Justin leaned back in his chair. "Fiancé?"

Roxanne walked to the edge of the patio. She leaned against the railing and tucked some hair behind her ear. She looked six stories down and watched the trolley rumble along. "We didn't get married." She took a breath and focused her gaze on a woman walking on the sidewalk. "Because he died."

Justin stood and from behind her put his arms around her waist. She leaned back against him.

Her eyes were tearing but she kept her voice steady. "It was...I still can't talk about his death. And there hasn't been anyone since then." She turned to face him, and caressed the necklace around her neck. "I loved him; I'll always love him. We met on the first day of med school...were best friends. He was everything to me." She opened the locket and showed the picture to Justin.

He regarded it, a slight frown on his lips. He pulled her close and hugged her. "I'm so sorry. I knew you were struggling with something but I didn't know it was that terrible." He used his sleeves to wipe her tears and lightly kissed her forehead.

"A simple appendectomy. He became septic post-op day three." Roxanne let the tears flow. "They did a last-ditch surgery to save him but he coded and died while they tried."

Justin pulled her close again and stroked her hair.

She leaned against him, her fingernails light against his back, and then she pulled away. "That lasagna should be cool," she said.

CHAPTER FIFTEEN

⌒

*C*lean shaven and sober, his platinum blonde hair slicked with gel, D.K. strode into the first-floor conference room five minutes late. He was experienced with these reviews after six years in California, these good 'ole boys in Tennessee would be a breeze, he thought. Everyone on the committee was seated on one side of a rectangular wooden conference table, talking softly and drinking coffee.

"I'm not quite sure why you've asked me to this meeting," D.K. said. Wearing clean scrubs and a freshly pressed lab coat, he took a seat at the table across from them and leaned his formidable body forward. Seated directly across from him was a man with a bald white head and glasses. D.K. presumed he was the president of the med exec committee. Looked the part, he thought.

Next to him was a young female administrator in a short skirt, black heels and dangling earrings. He imagined lace panties underneath her skirt. He flashed a smile at her that emphasized the faint dimple in his chin. She returned the smile but it barely reached her eyes before she looked away.

The operating room director to the left of her was a pig, he thought. She didn't deserve his acknowledgment. Seated next to her he recognized the Chairman of Surgery, Dr. Brian Armstrong.

"Well, first of all Dr. Webb, thank you for taking time out of your hectic schedule to meet with us," said the bald man. "I'm Dr. Slater, the med exec president."

Right on script, he thought.

"You're welcome, if we could hurry it up though that would be best," he said, glancing at his Rolex. "I have a case to start in twenty minutes."

"Well let's get straight to it then. We have something serious we need to address with you. There was a case on Saturday, October 22. A single-level lumbar lumbar laminectomy and fusion on patient Mrs. Chelsey."

He passed around a stack of stapled papers to him and the others.

"Could you tell us, doctor, what happened here?"

D.K. flipped through the papers and held the post-op CT scans up to the light above him and said, "Straightforward lumbar laminectomy and fusion. Looking at her images, I can't tell you why she's not walking. It was a clean case." He shoved the papers back across the desk.

"Our chief neurosurgeon reviewed these images and examined her, as well. He believes the pedicle screw you placed penetrated the nerve root and even sheared her spinal cord."

D.K.'s gaze pierced Dr. Slater. These guys had nothing, he thought. All of this was a risk of surgery and they knew it.

"I didn't know she'd followed up with someone else," D.K. said, his voice low and steady. "Who authorized a transfer? She's my patient."

The operating room director cleared her throat. "Doctor Webb," she said, "the ICU nurses on duty documented multiple attempts to reach you post-op to no avail. They eventually had to page the neurosurgery chief."

"Where were you post-op?" Dr. Armstrong said.

D.K. remembered the blonde from the rooftop party and made a mental note to call her. She was ferocious in bed, he thought. "I never got a single call from the unit," he said. "Where I was is irrelevant. Maybe your nurses called the wrong number."

"If you flip to page fifteen, you can see our phone records prove otherwise." The director replied, pushing the stack of papers back to him. D.K. gave her a look of disdain as he flipped to page fifteen.

"Then something was wrong with my phone. Like I said, I didn't receive any calls."

"What about your pager?" She coughed again and took a sip of water. "Was it also broken?"

"I turn it off when I'm not on call. And I wasn't on call."

"Dr. Webb, if you want to keep privileges at this hospital you have to keep your pager on," Dr. Slater said. "Especially when a surgical patient is unexpectedly admitted to the ICU."

"Okay, will do," he said and stood. "We done here? I've got that case to start."

"Excuse me, if you would sir, please sit," Dr. Slater said. "This was an egregious case. And there *will be* more investigation into it. An outside physician reviewer that our legal counsel has arranged is currently reviewing it." He adjusted his glasses and looked down at another chart. "But there's another case we need to discuss that has us even more nervous." Once D.K. sat, he handed him another stack of papers. "This patient had a simple fusion and you got into significant bleeding. Can you tell us please what happened?"

"I did what I'm trained to do. I made an incision in her obese neck, and while cutting, I inadvertently nicked the vertebral artery. I also stopped the bleeding appropriately with thrombin, pressure, and ultimately primary repair."

"The anesthesiologist on record told us you refused surgical assist from vascular," Dr. Armstrong spoke loudly. "Is that how you were trained in California? To refuse assist?"

"I didn't need it."

"That patient can't swallow now. She had a stroke."

"If Dr. Roth had kept up with the blood, there wouldn't be a complication," D.K. said, leaning back in his chair.

Dr. Armstrong leaned forward. "Well, I know Dr. Roth's work personally, and she's vigilant. I can't imagine she didn't support the patient with blood and pressors."

"Apparently not well enough," D.K. said. "She's the one that needed the assist, not me."

The room was silent.

"Here's what's going to happen while both of these cases go under further review," Dr. Armstrong said. "We'll allow you to continue your practice, but for the next two months you'll require a surgical colleague scrubbed in with you. One of the neurosurgeons or their residents, or if they are unavailable, myself."

D.K.'s gaze remained steady on Dr. Armstrong. They were giving him a babysitter, just like they did in residency. "I thought you're an ENT, Brian. How exactly could *you* assist?"

"I'm only there to observe. And I did two years of neurosurgery before switching into ENT."

"Couldn't take the pressure?" D.K. said and stood. He buttoned his lab coat. "It's not for everyone."

"Clearly," Dr. Armstrong said and closed the folder. "It's not."

CHAPTER SIXTEEN

⌒

A patient with a square chin and a full set of dentures had wisps of silver hair on the sides of his head like tufts of a peacock. His clear eyes belied the eighty-nine years he'd spent on a farm as his gaze followed Roxanne's approach.

"Mr. Cole," Roxanne said. "I'm Dr. Roth with anesthesia. You're here for hip surgery?"

Mr. Cole shook her hand, his grip firm. "Lady! Your hands are colder than a well-digger's knee." He let go quickly. "And you don't have to yell. I'm old but I can hear ya."

She mirrored his smile and lowered her voice. "I have to place an IV. Do you have a preference in which arm?"

Mr. Cole viewed the needle in her hands. "How about your arm?"

Roxanne's laughter garnered a collective look of disapproval from nearby staff. Again, she lowered her voice. "My arm's not an option, I'm afraid." She spotted Justin. He nodded at her and walked to a patient a few slots down. Justin's head was lowered as he typed into his phone. A moment later her phone vibrated.

Let's walk pups after work again?

She smiled and texted back.

Perfect.

"Sorry about that." She quickly pocketed the phone but caught Mr. Cole's knowing expression.

"Your beau?" he said. "Kids these days...with their emails and texting."

"Mr. Cole, I'm hardly a kid." She sat on a stool and examined his right hand for a vein, wiping it with an alcohol swab. "What's wrong with texting, anyway? How would you let a girl know you wanted to see her after work?"

"I plum married her." He laughed again. "We were seventeen years old. And she was always at home when I got done with work. No texting required." Again, their laughter drew scowls from the staff.

"Dr. Roth, keep it down." Justin walked by, and winked at her. "Patients are resting here."

"Ahh, the boyfriend, no?" Mr. Cole whispered when Justin was out of earshot.

"Maybe. Let's finish this IV." She smiled. She had a blue latex tourniquet in her hand and was about to tie it around his right forearm.

"Ouch."

"I didn't even touch you yet," Roxanne said.

"I'm practicing."

As she placed the IV she reflected on Justin. The past two weeks at work had been light and she'd been getting home before sunset every night. Their walks along the river had become a welcome routine. Memphis was having a mild fall. The trees competed for beauty with their fall foliage of orange, red, or yellow. Her favorite was the prehistoric bright gold ginkgo, especially the magnificent one in the dog park they frequented. Lyla and Wrigley chased each other while their owners flirted and kissed.

Alfonzo came to Mr. Cole's stretcher as she finished the IV. "Hey Roxanne, you can go on home, you're pre-call for OB? I'll have Sullivan pick this case up."

"Go get ready for your beau," Mr. Cole said.

"Beau?" Alfonzo said.

Mr. Cole turned to Alfonzo. "That guy over there." He whispered, pointing across the room at Justin's back.

"Mr. Cole, I'm going to put you to sleep right now," she tapped his hand. "He's on pain medicine, an unreliable source."

"Wouldn't be a bad match, Ro-Ro," Alfonzo said. "Not bad at all."

The next night when Roxanne was on call for the labor unit, the call pager, known as "the bomb," squawked #911. She bolted from her call room to the nurses' station. It took her a moment to comprehend the scene in front of her. A woman in brown scrubs was convulsing on the floor; her right shoe was missing; she had a hole in the sock at the big toe. Four nurses encircled her. Two were attempting to place an IV: one held the twitching arm of the patient while the other stuck the vein. The other two were cushioning her head with a pillow. Roxanne recognized Susan on the ground, one of her favorite labor nurses.

"Get the crash cart!" Roxanne said. She crouched on the floor and turned Susan's head to the side. Susan's secretions flowed out of her mouth onto the side of her face, hitting Roxanne's hand. The nurses continued to restrain Susan and tape down an IV.

"Can I get some gloves?" Roxanne said. Wendy, the charge nurse, handed her a pair. Susan's pursed lips were tight, her face was blue. Roxanne took the ventilation bag from Wendy and forced oxygen into Susan's lungs. Susan's color improved, but the seizure was ongoing.

"How long's it been?" Roxanne said with a glance at Wendy. She was thinking how different Susan looked now compared with her baby shower a few months ago. How radiant Susan had been, how thrilled she was as she opened Roxanne's gift, the infant activity pen.

"It's been over five minutes," Wendy said. "I know she's got a history of seizures. Her husband's on the way in. He said she hasn't had one in years."

"Ask him about allergies. If none then let's push two milligrams of midazolam IV. We've got to break this."

Within moments of administration, Susan's brown eyes stared blankly out. Her body stopped jerking. Her breath became deep and regular.

"We need to call the ER. Get a stretcher. Let's take her down with monitors and oxygen. They can draw labs and load her with Dilantin." Roxanne relaxed and sat on the floor next to Susan, still holding her head to the side, and kept her left hand under the chin. She could feel Susan's breath against her palm. With her other hand she stroked Susan's curly red hair. When the stretcher arrived, the team listened to Roxanne for further instructions.

"On the count of three, let's lift her directly up and onto the stretcher." The five of them took a place next to Susan, who was still sedated but breathing easily. "One, Two, Three." While they transported her onto the elevator downstairs to the ER, Roxanne felt a woman's hand gently touch her arm.

"I'm so glad you were here today," Wendy said.

"I'm glad all of us were there. What if she'd been driving? Or by herself? At home with the baby?" Roxanne felt a sudden wave of nausea hit her. She gripped the guardrail of Susan's stretcher, leaned over, and focused on her breathing. *Must be adrenaline.* She looked around but no one seemed to notice. The elevator doors opened. The nausea intensified.

"Excuse me, I'll meet…I'll meet you guys in a few." She pushed the stretcher out of the elevator, and realized the bathroom was too far away. She spotted a yellow mop bucket down the corridor, and ran to it. The vomiting was projectile and inevitable. She continued to lean over the pail for assurance, not convinced it was over. She caught her breath.

Wendy came to her side. "You okay?" She handed her a tissue.

"Yeah," Roxanne said and wiped her mouth. "Must be the cereal from the break room. I thought the milk tasted funny."

Wendy laughed. "Around here that kind of behavior means but one thing, and girl, it is not caused by spoiled milk."

"Ha." Roxanne smiled and walked up a flight to brush her teeth in her call room. When she reached the top of the stairs, the nausea hit her again.

Roxanne's cycle had been sporadic her whole adult life; she rarely paid attention to its timing. She kept tampons in her purse and locker at work and forgot about it until she needed them. Mark used to say she was bad at being a woman. "How do you not know?" He would be asking her right now. But for the past five years, she didn't have much reason to pay attention. She couldn't remember if she'd had her period since her one night with Nick. *Surely I did*, she thought. *But when?*

When her shift in labor and delivery was over, she drove back downtown. The sun was rising behind her. She turned into the parking lot of a drugstore and sat in her car for a few minutes, then turned back out and went home.

With towel-dried hair, wearing jeans and her favorite T-shirt, she met Justin in front of her condo building. Lyla, leashed, led the way. Justin got out of his Jeep Wrangler, gave her a bear hug, and opened the passenger door for her. Mark had been a "Southern gentleman" as well and Roxanne found the door opening endearing. Roxanne and Lyla got in and the dogs greeted each other in the back seat.

Justin gave her a kiss on the cheek before closing the passenger door behind her. He took the wheel and put the car into gear. His silver widow's peak was partially covered with a brown knit cap, his hazel eyes focused on the road. Roxanne reached over and tucked a strand of his hair behind his ear. He smiled.

"How was call?" she said.

"Had some elective cases that went late. Then I helped the orthopedic team out with a couple of their patients in the ICU. Oh, I saw Webb too. In the men's room."

"And?"

"His locker's near mine." Justin's gaze was focused on the road. "He took a swig from this thermos in his locker. I couldn't see what he was drinking but I could smell it."

"Liquor?"

"Yeah. I mean he was right next to me and coughed, didn't even cover his mouth."

"What'd you do?"

"Texted Armstrong, but Webb had vanished by the time he showed up. You know Webb's sleeping with some sales rep too. I heard she came to the hospital last week. They went to a call room."

"Which rep?" She noticed her right shoelace was untied, again. She bent her knee and retied it.

"I don't know her. A pretty blonde. The guys, not me by the way, call her a 'bounce around.'"

"'Bounce around?'" She finished tying her shoelace.

"A girl, that bounces...from one doctor to the other. Looking for gold."

"That's a horrible thing to say, Justin. What do they call the doctors that sleep with her?"

"Fortunate?"

She smacked his hand.

"Not cool, double standards!"

"Forgive me." He glanced at her. "I promise I'm not a chauvinist pig. I don't bounce around, I swear."

They were on a completely deserted back road behind Shelby Farms Park. The Jeep bumped along the dirt path. The morning spring air hit her face, and she looked at him; his intense eyes, the way his jaw relaxed, how quick he was to smile. She hoped he was one of the good guys, despite that joke.

"Pull over." She put her hand over his on the stick shift.

"Why?"

"Just. Pull. Over."

The car came to the shoulder and halted. She unbuckled her seat belt, and crawled over to the driver's side, straddling Justin. His arms wrapped around her. She looked behind him and saw only trees and birds; no one was near. She held his face in both her hands and kissed him fully. As the kisses intensified, Justin reached around, his hands on her lower back and hips. He kissed her neck, his hands eagerly becoming familiar with her. Her bra unhooked in seconds.

Something wet hit Roxanne's left eye. Wrigley had both his paws on Justin's back and continued to lick Roxanne. She pulled away laughing, wiping her face with her T-shirt, exposing her flat stomach. "Your dog just cock blocked you Justin."

"Damn dog," he said, still gripping her hips. "You want to go to my house? My sister's not going to be home for hours." His voice a whisper as he kissed her neck. "Are you ready?"

She pressed her cheek against his. She felt some discomfort in her lower abdomen. *Is that cramping? Please let that be cramping.*

"Not yet," she whispered, into his ear. "But soon, I promise."

CHAPTER SEVENTEEN

Roxanne shook the wet fuchsia coat off her shoulders. It was too heavy for Memphis winters but good in the rain. It had been her favorite purchase in New York during the first winter of residency; the bright color lifted her mood. She hung it on a hook in the doctor's lounge then went to the control board and found Alfonzo marking up his operating room schedule in black marker.

"Roxanne, could you go set up for burr holes in room six? Add-on we need to cover."

"The patient up here yet?" she said, drinking the last of her morning coffee.

"Patient's on the vent so they haven't sent just yet. Post-op day three from a hip, fell at home, hit his head now has a subdural hematoma."

She pulled her hair into a scrub hat while she walked a few feet down the hall. She turned back, her hands holding onto the stethoscope that hung around her neck.

"Last name isn't Cole, is it?"

Alfonzo looked at the schedule and flipped to the back sheet. "Cole. How'd you know?"

"I pre-oped him for the hip. He teased me about Justin. Remember him?"

"Yeah, now I do."

"Who's the surgeon?"

"Webb. He's on call for emergency neuro."

"Poor guy, first he falls and now he's got Webb," she said.

"A second-year neuro resident can do a burr hole," Alfonzo said. "I'm sure it'll be okay."

She walked down the corridor to OR six and sat on the bench in the supply nook to put on disposable shoe covers. She wasn't going to throw away another pair of shoes because of that blood-letting surgeon. Any neuro resident can do a burr hole, she thought. How much damage could he really do? He just needed to evacuate old blood off the brain and Mr. Cole would be fine.

The operating room was being set up; a gowned and gloved surgical scrub tech had placed instruments onto a stand that was covered with a sterile drape. While Roxanne prepared her supplies, the room sounded more like a construction site than a quiet operating room. She turned to see the tech test the perforating drill.

Roxanne drew syringes of medications then went to pre-op. She spotted an inpatient hospital bed being rolled into the holding area. Mr. Cole's eyes were closed, an 8.0 endotracheal tube was in place, and his dentures were removed. He had two working IVs in his arms and an arterial line in his right wrist. She checked the monitor. The bright red waveform was visible; 124/63 with no pressors hanging. He was stable.

While she listened with her stethoscope for even breath sounds administered by a ventilator machine, she spotted Brian Armstrong, who was dressed in surgical attire, approach the foot of the bed. She took the stethoscope out of her ears. "What's up?" she said.

"I'm assisting on this case."

Roxanne walked to the foot of the bed and whispered. "Is this about Mrs. Welty's case?"

"Among other concerns."

"You want me to roll back? I haven't seen Webb yet, but if you're ready, I am," Roxanne said.

"I'll text him and let him know we're rolling."

Once Roxanne and the team had the patient on the operating table, Roxanne hooked the endotracheal tube to the anesthesia machine ventilator and turned on sevoflurane gas. They turned the OR bed away from the anesthesia machine ninety degrees to give the surgeons more room to operate.

D.K. walked into the OR after Armstrong.

"Roxanne, good to see you again," he said. "I'll need you to keep his blood pressure up."

Roxanne glanced at him and said, "Why don't you go scrub and let me worry about his blood pressure, D.K."

The tech washed the patient's head and covered it with a drape, and the surgeons scrubbed their hands in the hallway corridor. Webb walked into the room with his hands held up like a referee at a football game to keep them sterile. He pushed both arms forward into the blue surgical gown the tech held up for him.

"Let's drill," he said as he did a complete circle around in place and tied the blue belt of the gown around him. He was sweating, his surgical cap damp around his forehead.

Roxanne stood watching over the sterile drapes. She glanced at Armstrong, put her index finger to her right eye and tilted her head at D.K. Armstrong nodded. D.K.'s clear protective surgical glasses did little to hide his dilated pupils.

D.K. reached and grabbed the sterile surgical handle of the ceiling spotlight to focus the beam onto Mr. Cole's head. "Watch how it's done," he said to Armstrong. Webb made an incision on the left side of the head, just a few inches behind the hairline. He exposed the skull and used a retractor to hold the incision in place.

"Drill," D.K. said with his palm out. The tech tested it once more before handing it to him. He put the circular metal bearing against the patient's skull and bore down. Armstrong's gaze was focused on the surgical site as the sound of the drill filled the room.

"You're too deep," Armstrong said.

D.K. continued drilling.

"It's too deep!" Armstrong yelled over the loud drill.

Old blackened blood seeped out of the hole. The dura had been pierced.

Webb turned the drill off and turned his head slowly. "Never interrupt me while I'm working."

"Put the drill down," Armstrong said. "Now."

The surgeons looked at the now bloodied operating field.

"Suction," D.K. said. "I'm evacuating the clot. That's the purpose of this surgery for those ENTs in the room."

"You went too deep with the drill. You could've punctured the brain the way you were plunging." Dr. Armstrong bent forward and looked closer inside the wound. "You got lucky."

"Luck's got nothing to do with it," D.K. said. "Now, I'll close." Sweat dripped from his forehead onto the surgical field. He shifted his weight from left to right and swung the suction tip around in his hand.

"Irrigation," he said, and dropped the suction tip on the floor.

"No," Armstrong said, taking the irrigant solution out of the tech's hand and putting it back on the tray. "Step out of the room with me, please, Dr. Webb. Dr. Roth, I'll be right back in to close, if that's okay."

Roxanne checked the monitor and adjusted the anesthesia gas lower. "Vitals stable. Okay with me."

"It's not okay with me. You don't know how to close this, Brian."

"I'll call for neuro to assist if I need it. Now, please, step out of the OR with me."

"For Christ's sake…" Webb snarled as he ripped his blue surgical gown off and shoved it in the garbage. He threw his bloodied surgical gloves on the floor and pushed the OR door open.

⌒

"What's your problem man," D.K. said, his Viking physique towering over Armstrong as they stood in the sterile corridor. Two female surgeons were scrubbing their hands at the sink next to OR eight. They looked behind them at the commotion.

Dr. Armstrong signaled for D.K. to follow him to a more private alcove near the sinks. Armstrong spoke with a quiet voice. "You appear to be impaired. If you want to retain clinical privileges, I need you to go downstairs to employee health right now and get a drug test."

"On what basis?" D.K. crossed his arms.

"You're sweating profusely, and your pupils are dilated. You can't stand still and you almost drilled a hole into a man's brain."

"Says the ENT surgeon." D.K. spit into the wastebasket and wiped his face with the sleeve of his scrub top. "You don't know what you're talking about."

"Prove me wrong. Go downstairs right now and get tested. I'll call and tell them to expect you directly."

"You're going to owe me an apology and I'll expect it in writing." D.K.'s lab coat was on a hook by the sink of OR six. He put it on, walked away, and pushed the metal pad to open the automatic doors. He paced in a semi-circle in the hallway. Armstrong wasn't going to fall for his usual delay tactics. He needed a clean sample and he needed it fast. As a doctor he could go anywhere in the hospital; he just needed a plan.

He went to the sterile supply room and scanned his badge to unlock the door. The metal racks were filled with supplies; he walked through row by row of gloves, sutures, catheters, and foleys until he found what he was searching for. He took the specimen cup and pocketed it in the front of his lab coat.

He took the stairs down one floor to the telemetry unit. Those inpatient cardiac patients shouldn't have any narcotics in their system, he thought. He walked down the hall listening to their beeping heart monitors. He saw a standing huddle of three nurses in scrubs, and walked silently by them.

"You need some help?"

D.K. turned. The diamond earring triggered a memory. He was the dude Roxanne was with at the rooftop party. Douche bag, mind your own business, he thought.

"No, man. All good. Passing through." He walked quickly to the right hallway, out of their sight. Room 428, 430, 432…all doors closed. 434. The patient's room was open. An obese, middle-aged man was asleep in his bed. D.K. didn't see anyone else in the room but what he did see made him smile. A half-full urinal was hanging off the bed's handrail. He shut the patient's door and quickly looked through the chart at the foot of the bed. He read through the patient's medication list. Bingo. He was clean. As he poured some of the urine into the specimen cup, the patient opened his eyes.

D.K. smiled widely, masking his slight overbite. "Just sending it off for metabolites, sir." The man closed his eyes. D.K. secured the cup with the green lid and slipped it back into his lab coat pocket. Test this, he thought, and pressed the elevator button down.

CHAPTER EIGHTEEN

⌒

*g*eeta, seated in a black vinyl reception chair large enough to fit three of her, flipped through magazines with her legs crossed. Her ankle occasionally brushed against Suvir's as she fidgeted. The office building on the corner of Front and Jackson even smelled new; the walls were freshly painted royal blue and the linoleum hardwood floors showed no wear and tear. Floor to ceiling windows overlooked the Mississippi River; the Bass Pro sign on top of the iconic Pyramid was in her view. Geeta remembered when the Pyramid was an arena. She attended Memphis State basketball games there when Anjali was in grade school. However, Memphis State was now the University of Memphis, her baby was having a baby, and here she sat in a surgeon's waiting room because her body was falling apart.

The room was crowded with patients; most were her age and older. "I don't care if he takes Medicare. I'm not waiting another second for him," a man wearing suspenders told the receptionist before limping out. The television was streaming thirty-minute clips of medical topics and advice. Geeta and Suvir were lectured on the signs and treatment of heart disease, followed by diabetes, and finally, obesity, before her name was called.

In the exam room they waited another thirty minutes until the door silently opened and a man entered. He wore black pants with a turquoise button-down shirt, a thin tie in a deeper shade of turquoise, and a white lab coat with his name embroidered above the chest pocket. Dr. D.K. Webb. She recognized him from the waiting room portrait. His petite nurse followed him in, carrying Geeta's medical file and MRI images. She tacked the MRI images to a viewing board, illuminating them.

"I'm Dr. Webb." He shook Suvir's hand, then Geeta's. "Sorry to keep you both waiting. I had to do an emergency burr hole case at the hospital this morning. Saving lives can't really wait, can it? Could you sit on this table and let me examine you?"

Geeta moved toward the exam table. D.K. offered her his hand as she moved onto a step and sat on the exam table facing him.

"Where do you hurt?"

"My neck, it sometimes starts there and goes down my left arm."

"And how long have you had this pain?"

"Suvir, when was the Harahan opening?"

"October 22," Suvir said, checking the calendar on his phone. "Two months ago."

"I fell on the bridge during the fireworks display," Geeta said.

"Those were nice fireworks. Put your arms straight ahead of you." He showed her by lifting his arms up parallel to the floor. "Now, don't let me push them down." He put his hands over her forearms and pushed.

Geeta tried to keep her arms up. Her right side stayed lifted but her left arm fell to her lap.

He put his hands out. "Squeeze my index finger as hard as you can."

She could barely make a fist with her left hand.

He took out a metal instrument with a sharp point on it from his pocket. "Close your eyes and tell me when you can feel this."

She waited.

"Open your eyes."

The sharp needle was firmly pressing on her left pinky.

"Look, let me show you both something." He motioned for Suvir to come closer. "You see the muscle on her palm near her pinky is smaller, compared to her right hand? She's lost muscle, it's atrophied."

"Will a block help?" Suvir said. "Her physical therapist thought it would."

"You can try nerve blocks, but they don't fix the actual problem." He pointed to the MRI images. "Now, look at this." He stood and pressed his pen to an image and glanced at Geeta. "This white line here? That's swelling, and it's all throughout your spinal canal." He pointed to a gray triangle. "And that's your fifth cervical disc compressing your spinal cord, on the left."

Suvir stood next to her and squeezed her right hand.

"A block is just a temporary measure," D.K. said. "You need surgery."

Geeta's eyes filled with tears.

"I need to think about this...when are you talking about exactly?"

"We could fit you in next month," the nurse said. "I'll connect you with scheduling to arrange it, and we'll need to get you into pre-admission testing."

"And what happens if I don't have surgery, doctor?"

"Then most likely you'll start to lose all feeling in your left arm, just like you have in your pinky." Webb rested his right hand lightly over hers. "Trust me, you need surgery." He looked her in the eye and softened his voice. "Cured in one day. In before breakfast, home in time for dinner. It's minor surgery. I'll take good care of you."

CHAPTER NINETEEN

~

Staring at her ceiling fan, Roxanne could not sleep. She counted nine weeks since her night with Nick and was certain she hadn't had a period. Justin was on a medical mission to the Philippines during his winter break, fixing cleft lips on kids and performing thyroid surgery on adults. He'd invited her to do the anesthesia but she couldn't get the time off. His being away allowed her more time with her therapist to delve into her "abandonment issues." That's what the therapist said was her underlying problem: abandonment issues. Roxanne disagreed, her arms folded, when she was sitting in her therapist's office. "I'm not a toddler. I realize Mark died and didn't intentionally leave me."

"On some primitive level we remain children forever," her therapist replied gently. "Once you acknowledge that, and cradle your inner child, the sooner you'll heal."

Justin was returning before New Year's and they'd made reservations for dinner at an elegant steak restaurant with his sister. She joked with her therapist that she needed to be cured by New Year's or she would want a refund.

02:05 read her nightstand clock. She would have to be at work in five hours for Christmas Day call. She dreaded the thought of working with D.K. Maybe the med exec committee had gotten him admitted to rehab. She'd visited Mr. Cole in the hospital two days post-op from his burr hole surgery. He was seated in a chair eating breakfast. He smiled widely and asked about her "beau." She read the progress notes in his chart: No residual deficits. It was incredible he'd survived.

74

02:40. She gave up on sleep and stepped onto the cold floor.

I need to get a rug under this bed.

Unclothed and shivering, she walked to her dresser. "Lyla! We're taking a ride!" She put sweatpants and a sweatshirt on and stepped into unlaced tennis shoes without socks. Her glasses, fuchsia coat, and keys were by the door, as was her pup. Lyla's feathered tail swished back and forth against the foyer table as she pawed at Roxanne's legs.

A light rain was falling and the wet pavement reflected Beale Street's neon lights; the Rum Boogie Café sign flickered on and off. She eased her black Camry along the main thoroughfare. On one street corner two men with baggy jeans and no belts exchanged cash for a paper bag. A decrepit Oldsmobile crept behind her. Windows up. Doors locked. She kept glancing at her rearview mirror at the Oldsmobile and coasted to the first stop sign. She reached across the passenger seat and felt for the mace can in her purse. The Oldsmobile turned on a side street. The twenty-four-hour drugstore on Union came into view; the parking lot was empty except for a solitary security car. She pulled into the drive-thru pharmacy, opened her window and reached for the call light. Lyla moved from the passenger floor onto her lap and pawed at her for attention.

A heavyset Black woman with braids pulled back in a ponytail came to the window chewing gum with her mouth open. The clerk raised her overly plucked eyebrows.

"I need a pregnancy test, please," Roxanne said as she petted Lyla and gave her a kiss on the soft fur on top of her head.

"Which one?" The clerk looked behind her on a shelf. "We've got Clearblue, First Response, Confirm, EPT, Walgreen's brand."

"Can you pick the one that'll say I'm not pregnant?"

The clerk picked at her long acrylic fingernails and yawned. "So which one ya want?"

"Give me one where all I have to do is pee on a stick." She continued to pet Lyla's head. She turned back to the clerk suddenly and said. "And a box of condoms."

"We've got Trojans, Durex, flavored, non-flavored, ribbed… Magnums?" she said. "That's what my man uses."

"Whatever's the most popular," Roxanne said. Mark had used Trojans. She had no idea what Justin used. The clerk took Roxanne's credit card and a few minutes later handed it back to her with a white plastic bag.

"Test better be negative. That dog don't want no competition," the clerk said. "Merry Christmas." She closed the window before Roxanne could respond.

"All right." She pushed the dog back over to the passenger's seat floor, and Lyla whimpered. "Lyla. Be good, girl. Mommy might be pregnant." She returned home as cautiously as she'd left and was relieved once parked in the secure underground garage of her condominium. Lyla hopped out of the car and steered her toward the back door, pulling at her leash.

The rain had stopped and she let Lyla relieve herself in the grassy patch behind the garage. She took the elevator up, and her knuckles clenched the Walgreen's bag as she went to open her door. The only baby she'd ever wanted was Mark's.

She unlocked her condo door, kicked off her tennis shoes and collapsed on her bed with her fuchsia coat still on. She read the box; <u>First Response</u>. She opened the package, examined the stick, and read the directions.

<u>Pee on it for five seconds</u>.

Roxanne went to her kitchen and drank a glass of the aquifer tap water Memphis was envied for. She sat on her couch and flipped through the recent mock exam questions she'd practiced. The tape recorder she used to practice exams with was on the coffee table. She pushed the play button and grimaced with every "Uh" and every "Umm." The board reviewers would destroy her if she sounded this bad. Chris, a perfectly capable colleague of hers, had failed it three times and had to start all over—retaking the written boards and then again failing the oral boards before passing on his fifth attempt. "You have to practice *speaking* anesthesia, not reading it," Chris told her. "It's a completely different way of studying. Docs, we're not exactly the best at communicating what we do."

Petting Lyla, whose head rested on her lap, helped her slow her breathing. She went to the bathroom and positioned herself on the toilet. She tried to adjust her stream to hit the stick in the correct spot. She counted one

Mississippi, two Mississippi, three Mississippi, four Mississippi, and peed on her hand as she finished.

She lay the stick on the bathroom counter and washed her hands. She glanced behind her at her bedside clock. 03:23. She sat on her bed. Then she got up and walked across the room. Then she sat back down. 03:25. She opened her dresser drawer and pulled out a pair of socks. The soft cotton felt good on her toes. She walked to the bathroom counter and looked at the stick. 03:26. She watched a pink wave move across the indicator. It was working. Roxanne lifted the stick, and held it closer to the light fixture that hung next to the mirror.

Something appeared where the pink wave had been, one dark pink vertical line and something else. It was unclear, so she needed more light. She searched in her bathroom for a flashlight, yanking open all six drawers. She glanced up again at the light fixture to the left of her bathroom mirror. It was directly above her granite sink. She put the toilet seat down and stood on it. With her left hand holding onto the towel rack above the toilet, she bent her knee to climb onto the granite. She felt herself losing her balance and with the cotton socks, she had zero grip on the toilet seat.

She felt the air underneath her as she fell backward. Arms flailing, attempting to grasp the towel rack, instead, found the shag rug. "Eye yiey yiey! Son of a..!" She screamed.

She lay on her left side.

You're okay, you're okay. She calmed herself down. Her left hip was going to be so sore. She turned to look for the pregnancy test, and found it lying to her right. It had a bright minus sign at the end of it. She sighed. Her period came the next day while she was sound asleep in the hospital call room with an ice pack on her hip.

CHAPTER TWENTY

⌒

The Memphis Zoo's light show for New Year's had been her daughter's idea. She wanted an adult night out while they still could, before the baby arrived and before Geeta's surgery. They had been looking forward to the celebration, but the crowd was suffocating. The throng of humans, in kitschy holiday top hats and blowing party horns, was noisier than the acrobatic monkeys.

Geeta cursed herself for leaving her pain medicine on the kitchen counter. It hurt to turn her stiff and unyielding neck, so her entire body had to swivel to see the many light displays. As they walked under an archway of lights, Christmas music played as the lights flickered around them, and her left shoulder and scapula throbbed almost to the beat.

"I lost my scarf somewhere between the polar bears and the Ferris wheel," Anjali said, rubbing her pregnant abdomen.

Kohi took off his scarf, wrapped it carefully around Anjali's neck and tucked her black hair into her snowcap. "You have to keep warm," Kohi said. The cold dry wind had turned Anjali's brown cheeks pinker. "You always lose something, you silly one."

"I do not. I'm quite capable, Kohi."

"Okay, then give me back my scarf."

"The baby wants it." She pushed his hand off the scarf.

"Let's get some hot chocolate, you two," Geeta said. "For a sweet year and a sweet baby."

A co-ed, in screaming pink tights under a short skirt, stopped abruptly to take a selfie under the arch of lights. Suvir put his arm around Geeta protectively and guided her around the girl.

"Let's find that hot chocolate with a place to sit for the fireworks?" he said. "I don't want your mom getting plowed over again by teenagers."

"So the lodge. I think you can see them from any spot," Anjali said, her hand on her baby bump again; she was finally wearing maternity clothes at the end of her second trimester. From behind she resembled one of the co-eds, her long athletic build remained unchanged.

They passed a series of lights forming three Christmas trees, in a sequence that lit on and off. The lodge was crammed. Suvir and Kohi stood in a winding line while the women found a wooden bench outside and sat close to each other for warmth.

"Only fourteen more weeks, Mom."

"It's happening fast." She was glowing, her mother thought. With her good arm she stroked Anjali's long hair. "You're so beautiful."

"And you're nuts! I'm a whale," Anjali patted her belly. "I think I like Marie. After Grandma. But for her first name though, not her middle name."

It had been over a decade, but nothing, neither joy nor pain, was the same without Geeta's mom. Life was anemic without her. Colors less bright. She wanted to call her and ask advice about her neck surgery, to share in the excitement of Anjali's pregnancy; there were so many things she wanted to say to her mother. But most important, she wished her mom could have met the great-granddaughter that would soon carry her name.

⌒

Roxanne squeezed Justin's hand as they darted from the parking garage to the restaurant. He wore jeans and a black cashmere sports jacket; the green shirt accentuated his hazel eyes. "I'm freezing," Roxanne said tightening her black wool trench coat around her waist. Her black pencil skirt offered minimal warmth.

Justin wrapped his arm around her. "That's why I wanted to drop you at the door." He opened the restaurant door and guided her with his hand on her back. The dim entrance was full of waiting patrons, and holding Roxanne's hand, Justin maneuvered to the reception stand. A young hostess greeted them. She had blonde pigtails and wore a disposable Happy New Year tiara.

"Kirkland," Justin said.

"Perfect," she said, and retrieved two menus from her podium. "Follow me."

As they neared their booth Roxanne saw the back of his head, then the diamond stud in his right ear. He was seated next to Megan, his left arm draped behind her in the booth as he pointed to something on her menu. Two champagne glasses were half empty on the table in front of them.

Roxanne yanked Justin's arm. "What's Nick doing here?"

"Meg invited him," Justin said.

"Why?"

"They're dating. I thought I mentioned it. Remember he recovered her after her surgery? Afterward, he asked her if he could check in on her. They hit it off."

"He's dating his patient?"

"She was his patient for thirty minutes," Justin said. "He's a nice guy. She's happy."

"Of course," she said with a forced smile, her heart racing.

Nick stood when they approached. He wore khaki slacks and a tie with a leather jacket. His smile was as generous as the hug he offered her. "Hey y'all. Thanks for letting me crash the party."

Roxanne's shoulders relaxed as she returned the hug. When she pulled away, he gave her a wink. Maybe her secret was safe.

Megan smiled up at them. She was wearing one of the New Year's tiaras. "You have to wear one, too." She handed a tiara to Roxanne.

"Because I'm not enough of a diva." She wore the tiara, tucking her long curls behind her ears, and mocked a queen's wave. Justin helped her out of her trench coat and hung it on a hook on the side of the booth, then slid into the red-leathered booth first and she sat next to him.

"Your sister says you just got back from the Philippines, Justin." Nick took a sip from his champagne glass. "How was it?"

"Astonishing." He pulled out his phone and showed them a picture of a thyroid specimen displayed on a blue towel. It had a penny next to it to show its relative size. "We took this out of a lady. I swear it was bigger than a heart. It's so different doing surgery there. You just make do with whatever instruments they give you." He flipped through pictures on his phone. In the before pictures, the patient looked like she'd swallowed a baseball and it got stuck in the middle of her slender neck. In the after picture, her neck had sutures in it and her smile was as wide as her neck was long.

"How long did she look like that?" Megan said, incredulous. She took the phone away from him and used her fingers to zoom in on the before picture. "Couldn't they take it out before it got so large?"

"They don't have a functioning operating room in her town. The closest one was Manila and she couldn't afford to go to Manila." He put the phone back in his coat pocket and surveyed the plates of steaks being carried to tables. He held up his glass. "They don't even have drinking water." He took a sip, put his arm around Roxanne and squeezed her shoulder. "You should come with us next year. Nick, we need PACU nurses too."

"Count me in, I love an adventure," Nick said.

Roxanne looked away.

Two servers approached with a metal cart on wheels. A white cloth tablecloth covered it. Arrays of champagne bottles were on it, as was silver confetti and pink streamers. Helium balloons with *Happy New Year* printed on them floated, attached by colorful string to the cart.

"Champagne?" one of the servers asked Justin and Roxanne, while the other one topped off the two glasses on the table. "Your friends are drinking Prosecco."

"How about that sparkling red?" Roxanne said.

"You have any whiskey?" Nick said and gave Roxanne a telling glance.

Justin watched as she responded.

"That red would be fine, thanks." She handed her glass to one of the servers and looked at Nick. "I don't care for whiskey. At all."

"I pegged you as a whiskey girl," Nick said and buttered a piece of bread.

"Then you pegged me wrong." Roxanne scooted out of the bench. "Excuse me, I need to wash my hands."

⌒

Roxanne's heels clipped on the linoleum as she paced inside the empty restroom, furious. As she washed her hands, the door swung open and Nick strode in. His mouth held a faint upturn.

"What are you doing here?" Roxanne said.

"It's gender neutral."

"I mean why are you here, on a date with me and Justin?"

"I'm on a date with Megan. She invited me." Nick handed her a paper towel from the dispenser next to him. "Please don't hate me. It's all copasetic. We can all be friends, you know."

"And that whiskey comment? Was that supposed to be friendly?"

A peacock of a woman wearing a feathered coat and matching hat walked into the bathroom, saw Nick and marched right out, her coat flapping behind her.

"It's gender neutral," he called out as the door shut behind her.

"Swear our history stays buried." Roxanne's gaze pierced into him.

"He won't care, Roxanne. Just tell him and get it over with."

"That decision is mine, not yours. Now get out of here, it's the damn ladies' room."

⌒

Roxanne and Justin left his Jeep in the restaurant's garage; neither was safe to drive after each finishing almost a bottle of wine. They huddled in the back seat of the Uber.

"That was a weird night," Justin said. "Did you and Nick used to date or something?"

"Date? No. Come closer."

As they kissed, he reached under her coat and felt the silk over her right breast. She put her hand on the zipper of his jeans. After she looked to make sure the driver wasn't watching them in the rearview mirror she unzipped, and her fingers stroked him lightly over his boxers.

A look of surprise flashed in his eyes.

"Tonight," she whispered.

"Tonight?" Justin said.

"Almost home," she said and kissed him. It's time to move on, she thought. She didn't have abandonment issues, she reasoned with herself, and no one ever needed to know about her and Nick, either. And Justin, well, Justin was perfect. There was no reason to mess with perfect.

CHAPTER TWENTY-ONE

D.K.'s apartment smelled of sex. A couple was under a blanket on the floor, their activity obvious to the other partygoers. Half a dozen women in varying degrees of undress, most barely old enough to vote, danced while D.K.'s fraternity brothers from Ole Miss sat on the couch and watched. Trance music blared through the living room speakers and the room lights were off; the muted TV screen flickered behind the girls, as did the only lamp in the room. A half dozen empty pizza boxes were on the coffee table and the pile of cocaine on the foyer table had steadily decreased.

"Who's got the sevo?" D.K. yelled over the music. His shirt was off and the button of his jeans undone. His abdominal muscles looked stenciled in. His biceps were just as defined.

"Here, man." His best friend since grade school, Seth, tossed the metal cylinder of anesthesia gas to him.

D.K. shook it and took off the bright yellow cap, pouring the last drop onto his palm. "You parasites, where's the other one?"

No one answered. He went to his bedroom and saw a redhead holding a Kleenex to her nose, and a heavily bearded man had his mouth between her wide-open legs. Her eyes were dazed. An open bottle of sevo lay next to her on the nightstand.

"You Cosby'ing it bro?" D.K. went to the woman and pulled her green dress further up, exposing her large breasts. He cupped one and squeezed. She took a deep breath into the Kleenex. He reached into his back pocket and threw a condom on the bed. "Don't bareback this one. She looks like she's been ridden too much already." He picked up the sevo bottle, shook it, and threw the empty bottle on the floor. He'd have to raid the anesthesia carts again. No one monitored their carts in the unused operating rooms late at night, and the code on all of them was a simple 4-2-5-1; he'd watched Roxanne punch it in when her back was turned.

He went to the kitchen and rummaged through a drawer until he found a prescription pad. He wrote Seth's full name and birthdate on it and Hydrocodone 10/325, #30, refill 3. He signed it.

"Get this filled, bro."

"Dude, now?" Seth was nearly asleep on the couch.

D.K. sniffed a line of cocaine off the table and rubbed his nose. "Yeah, now. And when my side business grows you're going to do it a lot more often." He saw Crystal. She was wearing the white lace thong and matching bra he'd bought her, covered by a wife-beater shirt, black high heels, and nothing else. "And you, my goddess," he pointed at her. "You'll be hitting up pharmacies for me soon too." As he pulled her to him, she rubbed against him to the music. "You'll help score some narcs, right babe?"

"I'll do whatever you tell me to, doctor."

"That's a good girl."

On the TV, a comedienne was pointing to the Times Square crowd as they cheered, blowing horns and throwing confetti.

"It's time!" Crystal said looking at the TV. "Five, Four, Three…"

"Happy New Year!" The room erupted.

"Crank that up!" D.K. said and turned a knob on the stereo. The music vibrated and the floor shook.

The med exec could kiss his white ass, he thought. He took Crystal's bra off and the guys cheered. She did a little dance for them, her large breasts bounced under the wife beater.

"Come with me," he said. He pulled her into his home office and shut the door. "Quit your job. Become my full-time girl instead." She kissed him in agreement. It was going to be a year of greatness, he thought, as he bent her forward.

CHAPTER TWENTY-TWO

⌒

*G*eeta shivered in the hospital gown that gave little warmth or defense. Suvir stood next to her stretcher gripping her hand. He kissed her forehead at his usual spot, the heart-shaped birthmark above her right eye, and tucked her blanket in around her. Anjali wanted to come with them into pre-op but only one family member was allowed. "Go home, baby," Geeta had told her. "Dad will phone you when it's over."

"No way. I'll be in the waiting room. Come find me, Dad, when they take her to the operating room." She'd kissed her mom's cheeks and said, "You'll do great Mommy. I love you."

That had been three hours ago. She wished they'd eaten later in the evening. Maybe she wouldn't be as thirsty now that her surgery had been delayed.

Geeta saw a woman dressed in scrubs, with enormous blue eyes framed in silver glasses and waist-length dark curly hair, approach her stretcher.

"I'm Dr. Roth with anesthesia." Her face held a smile.

"I'm Geeta," she said, tilting her head. "My husband, Suvir."

Dr. Roth extended her hand to both. "Good to meet you."

The doctor went to the foot of the bed and opened up Geeta's medical chart. "I'm sorry for the delay today. I bet you're getting hungry."

"I'm more cold than hungry."

"Unfortunately, I can't feed you, but I can warm you up a bit." Dr. Roth took two blankets from the warmer cabinet behind her. She removed Geeta's cold blanket and placed a warm one on top of her. The second one she tucked above her head, cocooning her patient.

"Oh…that feels divine." Geeta smiled. "Thank you."

"You look like a little burrito." Suvir laughed and took out his smartphone.

"Don't you dare," Geeta said. "He's taken so many photos of me already this morning. I'm surprised he didn't take yours yet, Dr. Roth."

"I don't mind. But first let me get your history and physical."

Geeta answered a series of questions.

"So you're healthy," Dr. Roth said. "Now let me take a good listen to your heart and lungs. I'll have to uncover you a bit just for a minute. Good, they've already placed your IV."

Geeta sat up and felt the cold metal on her back. She took deep breaths in as instructed. The cold metal moved to her chest.

"Can you open your mouth wide?"

Her anesthesiologist peered into her mouth and frowned.

"Have you ever had surgery?"

"Just once…the C-section for my daughter thirty years ago."

"Did they do a spinal?"

"I think it was a spinal. I was awake for it."

Dr. Roth asked her to open her mouth once more and peered inside. She used her fingers to feel the contour of her neck and asked her to swallow.

"Can you move your neck without it hurting?"

"If I move it to the left it's agony."

"Can you move your chin up at all?" She demonstrated by extending her neck like a swan toward the ceiling.

Geeta tried. It was frozen. Any movement caused pain to shoot down her left arm.

"Okay. Your airway doesn't look the easiest to intubate. You've got a small mouth opening, decreased range of motion, and impressive incisors."

"I have impressive incisors?"

"You do. But I've seen a lot worse, and we know how to manage challenging airways. Your risk for a sore throat might be higher, but the surgery itself can cause that as well. Dr. Webb been by to see you yet?"

"We haven't seen him today," Suvir said.

"I'll go check out some meds for you and I'll be back once your surgeon's here and ready to roll. Any questions?" she said.

"I know you'll take good care of my girl," Suvir said.

"I'll do my best, I promise."

Once Dr. Roth walked away Geeta looked at her husband. "Is she a doctor or a movie star?"

"Maybe she's both." He kissed her forehead then her nose. "Almost as pretty as you."

"Fibber." Geeta smiled at her husband. She squeezed his hand. It would be all right, she thought. She was in good hands.

Roxanne noticed Brian Armstrong dressed in scrubs in the hallway talking to a group of residents, one of which was Justin. Justin gave her a discreet look and she smiled at him.

"Can you talk?" she asked Brian.

"Of course," he said and walked with her down the hall. He cocked his head slightly, crossing his arms. "What's up?"

"Are you scrubbing in on Webb's ACDF?" she said, pulling her hair into a ponytail.

"Can't. He's over two hours late. I was going to but I've got my cases to start in thirty minutes."

Roxanne noticed his entourage of ENT residents was watching them and she motioned with her head for him to follow her farther down the hall. As they crossed into the frigid sterile corridor she pulled a scrub hat out of her back pocket and tucked her hair into it.

"So which surgeon's supervising him?"

"I don't have anyone free now. But you can always call me. I'll scrub out of my case if you see anything suspicious."

Roxanne stared at him.

"Seriously? Do you think I'm just decoration in there, like I have time to call you in an emergency? I've got to *administer anesthesia*, I can't be a surgeon's supervisor too. You saw the guy! He almost drilled a hole in a man's brain."

Brian sighed. "I can try and find a neuro resident to scrub in, would that make you happy?"

"Happ*ier*," she said. "What will make me happy is for him to lose his privileges. Our patients deserve better."

"I'm working on it. The committee's evaluating him carefully."

"Yeah, so carefully that he goes unsupervised."

"Roxanne. He passed a drug test. We don't have proof that he's impaired. Just document everything you can, okay? I'm on your side, I want him out too."

"I hope it's before he kills anyone." She shook her head before walking down the corridor to the anesthesia workroom. She scanned her badge to enter and looked among the thirty metal shelves on wheels, with over a thousand labeled bins for all things anesthesia related. She quickly found the portable video laryngoscope in the corner and wrote <u>Glidescope, room 8</u> on the dry erase board near the door. When she rolled it into OR 8, the scrub tech, Mrs. Averyheart, and the circulating nurse, Liz, were both seated and looking at their smartphones.

"Is he here yet, Momma Roth?" Liz said, rubbing her neck near her birds in flight tattoo.

"Three hours late. Maybe he won't show."

The operating room phone rang. Liz listened for a moment while looking at Roxanne. "Okay, I'll tell them," Liz said. "No such luck," she said, hanging up.

CHAPTER TWENTY-THREE

◡

*g*eeta's surgeon wore the suit and tie he'd worn in clinic but his tie was loose, as if he's changed his mind about wearing it. His shirt was a slim fit and outlined his muscles. He didn't look like he had any pain anywhere, ever.

"Mrs. De Silva." He shook her hand and then Suvir's. "Sorry for the delay this morning. I got…tied up. You all set?"

"As ready as I'm going to be," she said. Her surgeon took a felt-tip marker out of his pocket.

"Left side, correct?"

"Yes." She felt a soft pressure on her left neck as he scribbled something on her.

Suvir had his smartphone out again and took a picture.

"Baby, stop with the photos," she told him.

"You will like these one day." He pocketed his phone again.

"Any last minute questions?" Dr. Webb said as he put the marker back in his coat pocket.

"So a four week recovery you said?"

"She should go home this afternoon and rest. Usually back to normal activities in two to four weeks. Do you have a follow up with me scheduled yet?"

"In two weeks," Geeta said.

Her anesthesiologist approached the stretcher. Her hair was pulled into a bonnet and she had a syringe with an orange label in her hand.

"Ready for a pocket full of sunshine?" Dr. Roth said, her hand tapping the scrub pocket of her shirt.

She noticed that Dr. Webb's gaze lingered in the vicinity of that pocket. It seemed disrespectful. She didn't blame him though. The woman was mesmerizing. She wondered if they were both single.

"Roxanne Roth," her surgeon said. "I get the pleasure of working with you again."

"Indeed," she said. She took a vial out of her shirt pocket and drew up clear medicine into a syringe with an orange label on it. She looked at Geeta. "You got your hugs and kisses in?"

Suvir leaned across the rail of the stretcher and kissed her on her forehead and lips. "You behave in there."

"Go get some lunch." She knew Suvir's smile was artificial. His eyes couldn't mask the worry. "I'll be fine."

"Love you, Geetadita."

Geeta felt something warm in her IV as her stretcher was pushed forward. She felt less tense and safe.

"I love you too," she whispered with a soft smile.

"How're you feeling?" She heard Dr. Roth's voice from behind her. "A little better?"

"Like a superhero."

She heard her laugh. It was distinct and soft.

"We call it liquid courage."

Geeta looked at the ceiling panels as they passed above her head. Her nurse was near her feet helping to steer the stretcher.

"I feel bad you have to push this stretcher. Is it very heavy?"

"You're like pushing a potato chip compared to most patients," Dr. Roth said.

"Truth," Liz said.

A gust of air conditioning hit her from above as they entered the bright operating room. Geeta sat forward in her stretcher. "Is this the room? Is this where it happens?"

"Yes Ma'am," Liz said. "That's Mrs. Averyheart. She's the scrub tech."

"Are all those instruments for me?" Geeta said as Mrs. Averyheart waved a sterile gloved hand from her position at the instrument table. Her stretcher stopped moving and she felt a hand on her shoulder.

"We're going to have you scootch over to the OR table. Stay on you back, and move over." Dr. Roth patted the table. It had a white pad covering it and a purple foam pillow for her head. "I'm holding your IV tube."

Geeta's legs felt heavy after the sedative she'd received, but she slowly inched over to her operating bed. The foam pillow cradled her neck, easing her pain.

"I need this pillow at home," she said.

She felt Dr. Roth lift her left arm off the bed and place a cold cuff around it. It was tight for a few seconds before it let up. She heard the monitors. Beep. Beep. Beep. As she felt a wave of panic rising, the beeping became faster.

"Okay, Geeta," Dr. Roth said. "Just take some slow deep breaths. You're doing just fine." Geeta felt a hand gently rubbing the top of her head. "I'll be here the whole time watching over you. You might feel more medicine burn in your IV for a moment, but soon you'll be asleep."

She sounded like a mother, Geeta thought, and was trying to tell her so but felt a heaviness in her eyelids. She drifted into blissful unconsciousness.

⁓

"You catch that, Liz?" Roxanne said after she'd pushed the propofol and was masking the patient, giving her oxygen and sevoflurane anesthesia gas. Roxanne made a mental note that she would later chart, easy mask ventilation. "She was starting to panic."

"I did; she was pretty calm until then."

Roxanne pushed succinylcholine to temporarily paralyze Geeta's vocal cords. "She doesn't look easy, I brought the GlideScope in," Roxanne said. Her left hand was holding the mask on Geeta's face, and her right hand was squeezing the bag connected to the anesthesia machine. "Let's look," she said.

Roxanne held the laryngoscope in her left hand. Next, she opened Geeta's mouth using her right thumb and index finger to gently pry it open.

Keeping Geeta's neck neutral in the pillow she placed the blade in carefully and looked.

"No view at all. Thought that might be the case."

She just as gently took the laryngoscope out and started to mask the patient again. "I'll look with the Glide."

Liz pulled the GlideScope closer to the bed so Roxanne could see its video monitor easily. Roxanne again scissor opened the mouth with her right hand and with her left she inserted the GlideScope's plastic curved blade. The fiberoptic view it gave was impeccable. She saw the vocal cords and carefully threaded an endotracheal breathing tube. Satisfied with the placement, she secured the tube and turned up the sevoflurane gas.

"All set," she said, placing her stethoscope back around her neck. "Now where's that...surgeon."

She taped Geeta's eyes shut to protect against any corneal abrasions, then administered some narcotics and acetaminophen through the IV. She placed a temperature probe under Geeta's armpit, the cable connected to her anesthesia monitor. As she and Liz were leaning over to hook up the hot air machine for Geeta's warming blanket, their backs facing the door, D.K. arrived in surgical attire.

"Well that's a nice view," he said. He placed his phone and pager at Liz's station.

Liz and Roxanne rolled their eyes at each other.

"Scrub your mouth while you're out there scrubbing your hands," Roxanne said.

"Don't be like that, I was just playing."

She rolled her eyes again and pointed to the scrub sink. "Go scrub, Dickie."

Once he walked into the hallway to scrub, she texted Brian Armstrong. Where's my neuro resident?

CHAPTER TWENTY-FOUR

D.K. stood at the scrub sink in the sterile hallway. He could watch Roxanne in the operating room through the Plexiglas window panel above the sink. She had her phone in her hand and appeared to be texting. She thought pretty highly of herself, he thought, calling him Dickie instead of D.K. Everyone from medical school knew he hated the name Dickie. Dickie reminded him of being bullied in grade school; he'd been a scrawny runt until puberty had kicked in. That Swiss Army knife had scared the bigger kids off of him, especially after he used it in a fight and poor Liam lost part of an ear lobe.

His right knee hit the panel under the sink to turn on the hot water. He put his hands in the stream. Damn, that's cold, he thought, yanking his hands out. He looked through the Plexiglas as he waited for the water to warm up. Roxanne should be flattered someone of his caliber even noticed her. She gave it up to losers like that nurse and resident but not to him? What chick didn't want a neurosurgeon?

As he watched her his anger boiled. How dare she speak to him as if they were equals. He hovered between Christ and the Devil. She needed to be put in her place and quickly. Screwing her would accomplish it. If she wasn't going to sleep with him, then he'd have to do some mind games instead.

He washed his hands in the now warm water while adding more and more soap. He smirked when the idea came to him. You have to know how to do it right in order to do it wrong, he thought. Maybe an occult bleed under the longus colli muscle, slow and steady, would humble Roxanne up.

⌒

D.K. seemed tame today, thought Roxanne. He wasn't sweating or fidgeting. "Why're you still standing?" he said, looking at her over the blue drapes, his gloved hands hovered over Geeta's neck. "Anesthesia's usually on Facebook by now."

"And most surgeons are usually too focused on surgery to notice what anesthesia's doing."

"Everyone notices you." D.K. appeared to be smiling under his mask, the corners of his eyes wrinkled.

Roxanne said nothing, but remained standing. She watched his hands. Two hours into the case everything appeared normal. Mrs. Averyheart was handing him the usual instruments. The field looked clean, no abnormal bleeding. Maybe D.K. decided to give up drugs and be the surgeon he was trained to be. She knew he was intelligent enough; he'd aced every class in medical school. He could be a great surgeon, if he was clean.

But then again, his eyes. His eyes caused her concern. They were devoid of compassion.

Liz motioned with her index finger for Roxanne to step closer to the anesthesia machine and leaned into her ear to whisper. "Dr. Armstrong called back. He said he's sorry, but he was called to an emergency."

"It's almost over, anyway," Roxanne whispered. She looked over the drapes and raised her voice, "Are you not putting in a drain?"

"It's dry. She doesn't need it."

A lot of neurosurgeons didn't put drains in on a single-level neck fusion. Roxanne wasn't concerned.

D.K. placed Steri-Strips on the closed wound then stepped away from the operating room table. He pulled his sterile gown off in one quick motion by pulling it forward and tearing it. His gloves came off as well and he placed both gingerly in the red basin by the door.

"I'll be in the lounge," he told Liz, who was at Geeta's side undoing the Velcro safety straps from around the abdomen. "Thank you, Roxanne, great teamwork." He nodded to Mrs. Averyheart and Liz and walked out.

As Roxanne began to emerge Geeta from anesthesia, she watched her vitals carefully. She needed Geeta to be wide awake before taking the breathing tube out as it might be a challenge to get it back in. The airway would normally be a bit swollen after this surgery. She'd given her some steroids to help mitigate it.

Roxanne stroked Geeta's head and watched as Mrs. Averyheart and Liz counted the sterile laps one final time. Once accounted for, Mrs. Averyheart broke the sterile field down, taking down all the blue drapes.

"Geeta?" Roxanne said. Geeta's heart rate was slow, and she was breathing through the tube, slowly and deeply. "Geeta, can you open your eyes for me?" Geeta opened her eyes. "Good job." Roxanne leaned forward and held Geeta's right hand. "Squeeze my hand. Squeeze."

Geeta squeezed.

Roxanne took a syringe and deflated the endotracheal cuff and watched Geeta's breathing for a few more seconds. Satisfied, she pulled the tube out of Geeta's mouth.

"Good job, Geeta. We're all done."

Geeta smiled before falling back to sleep.

"Let's go," Roxanne said.

As they entered the recovery room, Nick waved them to his slot.

"New Year's was fun," he said while he hooked up his monitors to Geeta. "I swear, I'm still full."

"Yeah," Roxanne said. "It turned out to be a great night."

"I told you not to worry."

Liz was listening and watching their exchange. When they both noticed her, she gathered her papers and walked out. Roxanne walked to the head of the stretcher and reassessed her patient one last time. Geeta's eyes were closed and she was breathing easily and slowly. One more glance at her vitals on the monitor and she was convinced all was okay.

"I'll be in the anesthesia lounge if you need anything. Case went smoothly. I ordered Dilaudid if she needs it."

"Have a good lunch," Nick said and started his charting.

⌒

Alfonzo was eating at the boardman's desk. His operating room schedule was on six printed pages, his scribbles in black pen all over them. She knew his method. An X over a case meant it was done, a line through it meant it was underway.

She reached over his shoulder and pointed to her case on his schedule. "Done with Webb," she said. "It went surprisingly well."

"Excellent," he said as he marked an X over her case. "The coffee's fresh, they just brewed it."

"Thanks." Roxanne poured herself a cup. "Has Jamal been behaving lately?" Jamal was Alfonzo's son; a precocious mini-Alfonzo, with bright brown eyes and a permanent mischievous grin.

"Have I told you the Honda story?" he said, eating a barbeque sandwich and coleslaw from the cafeteria.

She shook her head.

"Last week we get a phone call at home from a car salesman at Honda asking to speak to Jamal." Alfonzo looked up at Roxanne. "I said 'Well, Jamal isn't home right now, can I ask why you're calling?' The salesman proceeds to ask me to *tell* Jamal he's received his online request, and that he has the car ready for him. So I said, 'That's wonderful man, but Jamal's only six years old.'"

Roxanne laughed. "You better start hiding your credit card!"

"So I find Jamal, and tell him we're not buying a Honda, and not to give out his personal information online. And do you know how that boy answered me?"

"I can't wait."

"That's okay Dad, I want a Lexus anyway." Alfonzo wiped the barbeque sauce off of his fingers. "That damn kid. I swear he has no fear."

"Fearless isn't bad, in and of itself."

"Oh, it's bad. He's going to be a spoiled little shit if I don't reign him in now. One day you'll learn what..." A loud buzzer was heard before the code alarm went off. "Anesthesia stat to PACU." A woman's voice repeated on the overhead speaker.

Alfonso and Roxanne darted to recovery, which was down the hall from their lounge. Four nurses had surrounded one patient.

Geeta!

She was gasping for air and had a look of sheer terror in her eyes. Her neck was swollen at the incision site; a large blood clot had formed and compressed her airway.

"Jesus H. Christ," Roxanne said and went straight to the head of the bed. "I need an Ambu bag. A hundred percent oxygen," she said as she put on a pair of gloves. Then she spoke into Geeta's ear. "Geeta, it's Dr. Roth. We're here with you. It's going to be okay, I'm giving you oxygen now." She placed the mask on Geeta and started to bag her. Geeta thrashed trying to sit up.

"Nick, cycle her blood pressure every two minutes. Someone call Webb stat. We need to take her back and evacuate the clot." She continued to mask her thrashing patient. "Geeta, calm down, honey. Calm down. Nick, I need restraints."

Alfonso spoke into his cell. "We need an empty OR and team stat. Bring back bleed for Webb."

Geeta's vitals were tanking. Her oxygen saturation was falling despite the one hundred percent oxygen. "We need to get her intubated. It's compressing her trachea," Roxanne said. "And where's Webb?"

"I've paged him twice, and called his cell," Liz said. "He's not answering."

"Call Armstrong," Roxanne said. "Get the difficult airway cart in here. Get me the GlidesScope. Call for a Vent."

"I'll draw propofol and succ," Alfonso said, rummaging through the medicine tray.

"I'm going to look without it first. She wasn't an easy airway to start with." Roxanne looked behind her to assess the vitals on the monitor. The heart rate and blood pressure were low. "Push atropine, Alfonzo. It's pulling on the carotid bodies."

"Armstrong's on the way," Liz said. "What can I do?"

"Get me suction," Roxanne said. "Let's have a look. We have got to keep her breathing on her own no matter what."

Geeta's limbs were now restrained with thick foam cuffs with nylon straps tied to the bed, but she wasn't fighting anymore. Her body was flaccid, a worsening prognosis. Roxanne took the GlideScope and placed it in Geeta's mouth but this time the view was gone. She saw no decipherable structures; everything was swollen and nothing was where it was supposed to be. She couldn't tell where the glottic opening was to the lungs.

"I've got nothing," she told Alfonzo, and took a deep breath. She looked again at the only place that made sense. She placed the breathing tube where the bubbles from saliva seemed to originate.

"Listen for breath sounds," she told Nick while Alfonzo hooked up the breathing tube to a detector. Nick had his stethoscope in his ears and was listening to the chest; he looked at her and shook his head. The detector didn't change colors.

She pulled the tube out of the mouth and continued to bag the patient, forcing oxygen into her lungs the only way she could. Even that was becoming difficult as the blood in the neck had further compressed the airway. She placed an LMA. It sat above the cords and was helping her get air in the lungs. She turned behind her and looked at the vitals. They were tanking again.

"We need more atropine. And I need a damn surgeon."

"We're here." She saw Brian and Justin putting on gloves. Brian stood next to Roxanne and placed his hand on the massive neck swelling. "Let's head back and evacuate. Did you try and intubate?"

"It's a mess," Roxanne said. "She's so swollen I can't make out any structures. I was going to try with the scope next."

"Let's get her into the OR and prep and drape," Brian said. "I'll need a trach kit."

Geeta was becoming unrecognizable. Her eyes were closed and her breathing shallow. Her neck looked like a blue football had grown under her chin. As they were about to push her stretcher to the operating room, the heart monitor alarm went off. Roxanne studied the rhythm. Geeta's heart was no longer sending signals to contract. It was in a rhythm unsustainable for life. If Geeta's chest was open, her heart would look like worms moving in a bag.

"Feel for a pulse." Roxanne hollered out. "We need to shock at 200."

The team scrambled to place the defibrillator pads on the patient's chest.

"Clear?" Roxanne said. No one was touching the patient. Some held their hands up in the air as proof. "Shock!"

Nick pushed the button on the defibrillator. Geeta's body convulsed. The rhythm didn't change.

"Start chest compressions!" Roxanne said.

Justin leaned over the patient, both hands flattened on her chest, pumping her blood for her.

"Push epi," Roxanne said.

Nick pushed epinephrine into the IV. The heart monitor showed a slow junctional rhythm. "Hold compressions. Feel for a pulse."

Alfonso felt for a femoral pulse in her groin. Nick felt for a pulse in the right wrist.

"None," said Alfonzo.

Justin continued the chest compressions while Roxanne tried to force oxygen into Geeta with the Ambu bag and LMA. It was becoming impossible.

"Prepare to trach," said Brian. "Prep the neck, now."

"I'll keep looking with the scope until you're in," Roxanne said. "Alfonzo, run it while I try."

"Get vasopressin in line," he told Liz. "Nick, swap with Justin on chest compressions."

She took out the LMA and placed her hand in Geeta's flaccid mouth, while holding the scope at Geeta's tongue. Roxanne held the scope in her left hand and maneuvered it with the controls in her right hand. "Suction!" she said. Liz hooked the suction up to the scope. Looking in the scope, Roxanne again saw only blood and swelling of the airway structures, but when Nick pressed down on the chest she could see bubbles. She advanced the scope toward the bubbles and threaded the breathing tube in.

She pulled out and connected the tube to the Ambu bag. The detector changed colors from yellow to blue. She took her stethoscope off her neck and listened to Geeta's chest. She was in.

"Okay, we have an airway." The monitor showed a functional rhythm. "Do we have a pulse?"

Alfonzo pushed on Geeta's groin with his finger. "We have a pulse."

"Roll," said Roxanne and the team pushed the stretcher toward the operating room.

Roxanne looked over the blue drapes as Brian, Justin, and a senior neurosurgery resident opened Geeta's incision. They'd removed a massive blood clot but the area kept bleeding. Roxanne pushed resuscitation medications and started infusions; Alfonzo helped her keep up with blood products. They spiked the fourth unit of blood, but the blood pressure was barely holding up.

"Did Webb respond?" said Dr. Armstrong.

"No," said Liz. "Who else can I call?"

"Keep trying the chief of neurosurgery and also call vascular." Dr. Armstrong pushed gauze against Geeta's neck, holding his hand tight against her to compress the bleed. "I don't know where it's coming from," he said to Justin. "We've bovied everything and it's still oozing."

"There's nothing left to clamp," said Justin. "What did Webb do in here?"

"Liz, get us some more thrombin," Brian said.

An alarm monitor sounded. Roxanne and the rest of the team looked at the heart rhythm and saw a flat line.

"Asystole. Justin, start chest compressions!" said Roxanne. "Liz, document."

Alfonzo pushed epinephrine through the IV again.

⁓

The pharmacy team had entered the OR and replaced the resuscitation drug trays twice. Nurses and techs had rotated through, offering fresh hands for chest compressions.

"Push atropine again," Roxanne said, looking over the surgical field.

"It's been 70 minutes, Dr. Roth," Liz said quietly.

Alfonzo put his hand on Roxanne's shoulder.

"Hold compressions," Roxanne said. Justin stopped the chest compressions and took off his mask, his expression full of sympathy.

Roxanne felt one last time in Geeta's wrist and then her groin. There was no pulse. The monitor showed the same flat line. She took off her stethoscope and listened for a heartbeat. The chest was silent. She looked at the clock on the wall and pulled her mask down. "Time of death. 15:52."

CHAPTER TWENTY-FIVE

⟡

"Excuse me," Roxanne said, and walked out of the OR. She went to the ladies' room, keeping her gaze down. She held it together until the restroom stall door closed. Memories flooded her. The look the surgeon had on his face as he told them Mark had died. His mother's wail. She wept until she heard someone enter the room. She waited until they walked out and then went to the sink. As she washed her face, she looked at her reflection. Her eyes and cheeks were red. She took a few calming breaths. She tucked her hair back into her cap and took off her glasses. With a tissue, she wiped Geeta's blood off of them.

She resolved right then that she would make it her mission to get Webb's medical license revoked. If she had to go to the *Commercial Appeal,* bang on the doors of the med exec's homes, drive to Nashville and yell at the medical state licensing board to be heard…whatever it took. That lunatic drug addict was going to pay for this.

She returned to the operating room and saw Dr. Peterson, the pathologist, preparing Geeta's body for the morgue. An autopsy was standard for a death in the OR. They had moved the body onto a stretcher and covered it with a sheet. Brian walked over to her and in a low voice he said, "I should've listened to you. He should've been supervised."

"Has he even called back?" she said, looking around the room. Justin had come to her side and held her hand. She squeezed it.

"No," Liz said. "The last he was seen or heard from was when he walked out at the end of the case. I've documented in multiple places in the chart every call made to his phone and pager." She'd been crying as well; her mascara was smeared and her eyes were bloodshot. Her neck was wet from tears, as if the three tattooed birds had been crying as well. Roxanne hugged her.

"I don't know what else we could've done for her," Liz said and shook her head.

"Webb should've put in a drain," Justin said. "She needed one."

"We're going to take her downstairs now," said Dr. Peterson. "Unless you prefer the family to see her up here in a viewing room. I can cover the neck, make her presentable."

"Up here, yes," Roxanne said. "Thank you for doing that. What about a chaplain? To come with us to tell the family?" She remembered a chaplain was there when they were told Mark died. "No one told them yet, right?"

"I was waiting to tell them together," Brian said.

⁓

The family waiting room on the first floor had laminate wood flooring and vinyl sofa chairs. Wall hangings of sunflowers were juxtaposed with a magazine rack of old issues of *Glamour* and *People* magazine. The TV was on a local station and Anjali and her dad passed the time watching the morning talk shows followed by games shows and soap operas. Kohi had an important trial and Anjali had insisted he go. But as the minutes turned to hours, she wished she hadn't.

Every hour the yellow rotary phone in the family waiting room had rung for them. A nurse named Liz told Anjali around noon that her mom was resting comfortably in the recovery room. During the next call Liz said there had been a complication and they had to take her mom back to the operating room. An hour later she told them her mom was in critical condition and the surgeons were working. Then silence. They hadn't heard from anyone in over two hours. No one at the desk could tell them anything except to be patient.

And then a man and a woman in scrubs arrived; their faces grim. The woman, a stunning brunette despite bloodshot eyes, walked straight toward Suvir. Anjali stood up, her hand, a reflex, patted her baby bump. "Dad. Doctors are here." Her father stood.

"Dr. Roth. Can you tell me how she is?" Her dad shifted his weight from left to right, his fingers steepled in front of him. He was biting his lower lip. The other families in the busy room became quiet, uncertain of what was happening but understanding it was bad.

"Mr. De Silva. This is Dr. Armstrong, chief of surgery. Will you follow us please?" Anjali held her Dad's hand as they walked behind the doctors. When they entered the smaller private room with a couch and four chairs, they saw a tall balding Black man in a white alb with a clergy collar.

"Oh God," Suvir said. "What happened? Where's my wife?"

It was as if everything was in slow motion. Anjali heard the woman say words like "complications, we did everything, we couldn't get her back." The man in scrubs said something about "uncontrolled bleeding." She stood looking at them. Nothing they said made any sense. Her mom was healthy. This was routine surgery. What happened?

"I'm sorry," her dad said to the man in scrubs. "I don't understand what you're saying. Who are you again? Where's Dr. Webb?"

The chaplain, with gentle eyes, came closer. He put one of his large hands on Suvir's shoulder. "Your wife has passed on. She died."

The woman came to Anjali's side and rubbed her upper back softly.

"I'm so sorry," the woman said.

Her mother had died. Anjali held her belly, and the baby began moving inside. This couldn't be real. How could her mother be dead? This was routine surgery! How was she going to raise a baby without her mom? A sudden noise, indistinguishable, almost feral. Tears welled in her eyes as she found the source. In thirty years, she had never heard her father cry.

CHAPTER TWENTY-SIX

*J*ustin and Roxanne passed framed portraits of white men along the corridor wall; previous CEOs of the hospital, each smiling, each wearing a suit. A female janitor was mopping the linoleum floor and had placed a yellow caution sign with a stick figure falling in the middle of the hallway. It partially blocked their path to the physicians' parking lot.

"Y'all be careful," the janitor said. "It's slippery."

Roxanne slowed her pace.

"It was so hard to see her daughter," Roxanne said. "She's pregnant with her first child and I failed her...I failed to keep her mother safe."

He put his arm around her as they continued walking.

"D.K. did it on purpose," she said.

"There's going to be an autopsy and a review board looking at the case. He'll have to answer to all of it."

"If he ever answers at all. Where the hell is that murderer?" She pressed the down button outside the elevator. "Who performs surgery and then doesn't answer his phone and pager? I'm telling you, this wasn't an accident."

When they got to her car, she gave Justin a long hug and he held her close.

"I miss Mark so much," she said, trying to slow her breath.

"I'm so sorry." He kissed the top of her head.

They held each other in the parking garage. Roxanne's tears created a wet spot on Justin's jacket. He pulled his thick wool scarf off and gently wiped her face.

"I don't want to ruin it," she said, sniffling.

"Shush. Megan knitted me this. She'd want you to use it." He put it against her nose. "I'm going to drive you home and draw you a bath. We'll have some wine. We both need it."

"And your car?"

"We'll figure it out tomorrow," he said and opened the passenger side of her car.

Once home, Justin made dinner and Roxanne relaxed in the tub with wine. She began to formulate a plan. By the time she'd finished her second glass she was furious instead of sad. She dried herself off with a soft white towel and put on her silk robe.

"We're going to get his privileges revoked," she said and sat with her laptop computer on the dining room table. "I'm going to write a detailed letter to the med exec, I'm going to cc it to the state medical board, and I'm going to threaten to send it the *Commercial Appeal.* That'll wake them up."

Justin stood over her shoulder and read as she typed.

"I'm writing everything that happened today, then I'm going to open Cole's and Welty's charts and document their cases too."

"I'll help you," he said, opening up his laptop. "I'll search through all his cases and look for any others with post-op complications."

"It'll be a confidentiality violation." She put her hand over his to stop him from typing. "We can't just open charts of cases we weren't a part of."

"So we follow every rule, while he follows none?"

"We're not on drugs. Or sociopaths. Or both." She typed into her computer. "We've got enough to go after him."

"In the ICU I rounded on a case, a laminectomy that woke up paralyzed." Justin started typing. "I can at least open that chart up."

"Okay, you find that one and I'll work on these."

When her letter was composed the crescent moon was high in the sky. She wondered briefly if it was too late to call but then decided this was one rule she'd break.

"Brian? We need to talk."

The next morning Roxanne, Alfonzo, and Justin were in pre-op seeing patients when they heard the effect of their evening efforts. "What do you mean it's cancelled?" A loud male voice reverberated into pre-op from the OR control desk outside. "No one cancels my cases without discussing it with me."

"Guess who," Roxanne said to Alfonzo and Justin and hung her stethoscope over her neck. "I'll be right back," she told her patient. She pushed the silver button on the glass door to exit and the three walked out of pre-op and found D.K. pacing. He wore scrubs and a white lab coat.

"You cancelled my cases?" he said to Roxanne, his voice low, walking toward her. "You don't get to simply cancel my cases without discussion. I'm in charge, not anesthesia."

Alfonzo stepped in between them, his broad shoulders inches below D.K.'s, and put his hand lightly on D.K.'s chest. He nudged him away from Roxanne. "The Department of Anesthesia has cancelled your cases today, not Dr. Roth alone."

"For what reason?"

"Maybe if you'd answered your phone you would know, Dickie," Roxanne said. "Where have you been?"

"None of your business where I've been, snowflake."

"This isn't productive, is it?" Alfonzo said quietly. Someone had called security and two armed officers were watching the scene as were several PACU nurses, including Nick. "Dr. Webb. A word?" Alfonzo said, and pointed to the doctor's lounge.

D.K. spotted the security men behind him. He muttered something under his breath and followed Alfonzo into the lounge. Roxanne and Justin walked behind them and Roxanne motioned with her head for security and Nick to join them. She texted Brian Armstrong as she walked.

OR doctor's lounge STAT. D.K. here.

The lounge was empty at this hour since most of the surgeons and residents were already in the operating rooms. The coffee pot was empty but the smell still permeated the room.

"Listen, this is what's going to happen," D.K. said, his arms folded across his expansive chest, his hands tucked under his armpits. "You're going to send for my first case and you're going to do it right now."

Roxanne took a deep breath and stood with a table between her and D.K. Alfonzo and Justin stood on either side of her. "Your patient, Geeta De Silva, died yesterday while you were nowhere to be found."

A flicker of concern crossed his face. "No one called me. What'd you do to kill her? She was fine when I left her with you."

"What did *I* do?" said Roxanne. "*I* resuscitated her, coded her, and watched her die from your cut!"

"She wasn't bleeding when I left, you must've been rough on her during extubation. You did something."

"I'll tell you right now, Dickie Webb, I know you cut her and left her to bleed to death." Roxanne was yelling now. "And the autopsy will prove it. You're an incompetent surgeon and a despicable human being."

A smirk formed on D.K.'s lips. "This coming from the hospital whore. Who are you currently screwing?" He looked from Justin to Nick. "The surgeon or the nurse?"

Roxanne's face flushed. Out of her peripheral view she saw Justin look at her and at Nick. She looked at neither of them. Her gaze became a dagger as it pierced Webb's cold, callous eyes. "*Whom* I spend my time with is none of your concern. But I'll tell you *what* I'll be doing with my free time. From now on, all of it, will be focused on getting your medical license permanently revoked. You belong in a jail cell."

The lounge door flew open and Brian Armstrong darted in, breathless as if he'd run a flight of stairs. He left his surgical scrub hat on and threw his scrub mask into the wastebasket. He approached D.K. "Dr. Webb. Your privileges have been immediately suspended until further evaluation by the med ex board."

D.K. shoved his hands in his lab coat pockets. "You can't just suspend me. On what authority?"

"I have full authority as chairman."

"No privileges, Dickie, so now you're trespassing," Roxanne said and pointed to the security guards. "Please get him out of here."

The security men flanked him. "Sir?" said the taller one, his hand on his holster. "We'll escort you out of the hospital."

D.K. smirked and spoke to Roxanne. "See you soon."

Roxanne's hands were trembling as D.K. walked out with the guards behind him.

"Good riddance, people," said Alfonzo. He grabbed one of the glazed donuts and took a bite. "He's done."

Roxanne kept her gaze on the table.

"I guess we should all get back to work?" Alfonzo said.

"I'll be there in a few." She couldn't stop her hands from trembling. She felt nauseous.

"Okay," he said and walked out. Brian followed Alfonzo, leaving only three in the lounge: Nick, Justin and Roxanne.

Nick cleared his throat. "I guess I'll head back to PACU."

"Wait a sec, Nick," Justin said. "Why would he say that? Are you sleeping with my girlfriend *and* my sister?"

Nick raised his hands, palms up and fingers spread. "This is between you and Roxanne. But no, I'm not sleeping with either of them, actually."

When Nick left, Roxanne raised her chin to look at Justin. She pulled out a chair at the table and sat. A half dozen donuts were on the table with the *Commercial Appeal* newspaper opened to the sports page. She pushed the donuts away. "Sit with me? Please?"

Justin pulled up a chair across from her, his hands clasped on the table. She wished he would reach out and hold her trembling hands but he didn't.

"Rox. Just tell me you didn't sleep with Nick."

"I can't."

Justin put his left hand across his forehead and rubbed it, his elbow on the table.

"You slept with Nick?" he said, shaking his head. "When?"

"It was one night..." she said. "Weeks before you and I ever started dating."

"Nick? The guy that's dating my *sister?*" He stood up and paced. "Why didn't you tell me when I flat out asked you on New Year's?"

"Because, why does it matter? It was before you and I ever dated."

"You lied to me, Roxanne! It's embarrassing. He's here, he's at my house. He's dating Megan." Justin took off his surgical scrub cap and threw it in the trash. "It's incestuous for Christ's sake. You should've told me." He walked out without looking back and when the door closed behind him, she found herself alone.

CHAPTER TWENTY-SEVEN

⌒

She spent the rest of her workday forcing pleasantries as she interviewed patients and avoiding eye contact with Nick in recovery as he worked silently. She didn't need to avoid Justin since he'd disappeared. *The hospital whore.* If anyone was a whore it was D.K, she thought, wishing she had yelled that at him when she'd had the chance.

She was disappointed in Justin; his lack of empathy astounded her. He hadn't given her a moment to explain her perspective; he only saw crimson. It was a character flaw she wasn't sure she could overlook. Mark would've at least heard her out. She texted her sister.

Having horrible day. Please meet after work? I need comfort; food and otherwise.

They dined at a local bar in Midtown. The ceiling was full of toothpicks that adhered to the ceiling from customers that had propelled them up with straws and forceful drunken breaths. The white walls were filled with graffiti; a tin can with Sharpies on each table encouraged it. The bar was filled to capacity. She heard a waitress laugh while flirting with the bartender. "Where's my beer, Bobby?" The waitress slapped him on the back pocket of his jeans with a rag.

"Man, I love these burgers," her sister said and bit into it. "I'm all ears and mouth. What happened?"

Roxanne picked up an onion ring out of a white wicker basket. "Short version? D.K. killed my patient and then he killed my relationship."

Her sister put her burger down and took a sip of beer. "I'm going to need the long version."

Roxanne played with the plastic edge of the red and white tablecloth. She explained all that had happened the day before with the death of Geeta, and her instinct that D.K. had killed the patient deliberately, and her actions to get him suspended.

"But what does this have to do with you and Justin?" Claire took another bite of her burger. "You said he killed your relationship."

"It's complicated, I didn't tell Justin, or you actually…"

The acne-laden waiter, wearing a University of Memphis T-shirt, approached their table. "How're the burgers?"

"World's best," said Claire and lifted up her beer bottle. "I think we need two more, please."

"Not me, thanks," Roxanne said. Once he walked away Roxanne confessed about her night with Nick.

Claire coughed on her beer. "Why didn't you tell me?"

"I was embarrassed," said Roxanne. "I've never done that before."

The waiter set a fresh bottle of beer on the table. "Do you need anything else?"

"I'll blow a toothpick your way if we do," Claire said and picked up a straw. Once he walked away, she spoke. "Let me clarify. Your one-night stand, the first guy you've been with since Mark, is a nurse with whom you and Justin both work?"

"And he's dating Justin's sister now," Roxanne said. "We actually double dated on New Year's."

"But what does Webb have to do with this?" Claire said. "You didn't sleep with him too, did you?"

"Oh my god, no. How could you say that?" Roxanne folded her arms on the table and buried her head.

Her sister reached over and stroked her hair. "Come on now, I was kidding. A little. Tell me."

Roxanne raised her head, resting her chin on her forearms. "In front of Justin and Nick and Alfonzo…Webb called me the hospital whore. He asked who I was currently screwing, Justin or Nick?"

"No he did not."

"Happened."

"How could he even know that?"

"The psycho has some radar on me. He saw me with Nick that night on the rooftop and another time out at dinner with Justin. Of course, you should see the women he takes out. One of them was practically naked."

"What is this, high school? Who you date is none of his damn business."

"Mark never would have walked away from me, like I'm some leper."

"Justin clearly doesn't deserve you then." Claire rubbed her chin and rested it in her hand with her elbow on the table. She chewed an onion ring slowly and took a sip of her fresh beer then spoke with a soft voice. "But even though he acted like a jerk, maybe it was because his ego was bruised. You know? We all have egos. You could've told him about it yourself? He probably was just hurt that was the way he learned."

"Said he was embarrassed."

"You were embarrassed, he was embarrassed. See, bruised egos. I'd give him a chance if he comes asking for one."

"I don't want to date such a fragile ego," said Roxanne. "I'm going back to celibacy."

Claire laughed. "Well your last emergence from the convent was quite dramatic, I got to say."

"Mean, just mean."

Roxanne looked through the tin can full of sharpies and chose red. In bold lettering she added her own graffiti on a vacant spot. <u>Beware of Dr. D.K. Webb.</u>

Roxanne stepped out of the elevator of her condo and walked to her apartment with her head down, her gaze on her phone. "Hey Rox." Justin was waiting for her outside her apartment door. His expression was difficult to read but clearly not one of happiness.

"Sorry to just show up," Justin said, rubbing his chin, his five o'clock shadow present.

"How long have you been waiting outside?" she said unlocking the door, not sure whether to invite him in.

"I punched Webb. In the face."

"You what?" Roxanne turned around. Lyla barked, her tail wagging. She took his right hand into both of hers, examining it.

"I used my left." He showed her his bruised and scratched knuckles. "I'm not going to use my dominant hand on that asshole. I couldn't let him get away with calling you that. So I caught up to him in the parking garage. He shoved me and said…" Justin stopped talking. "Never mind."

"What did he say?"

"It doesn't matter."

"Tell me."

"*I don't blame you for tapping that, bro, but when you're done with her, I want a taste.*"

"Oh my god, as if I'd let him." Roxanne pulled Justin and led him into her bathroom. "Down Lyla, down. Go couch, Lyla." Lyla walked with her tail under into the living room. Roxanne rummaged through the bathroom drawers for her first aid kit. "You don't have to fight my battles like I'm some helpless little child."

"I didn't do it for you. I did it for Geeta. I would've kept punching him too, but security came running back toward us."

Roxanne poured rubbing alcohol onto gauze; it smelled like the hospital. "I'm sorry it stings," she said, while carefully wiping at the abrasions on his left knuckles. She used her hand to fan it dry.

"Asshole just laughed and got in his car. I think he enjoyed the punch, enjoyed pissing me off. I spent the rest of the day at home, catching up on charts. I needed to calm down."

"I should've told you about Nick," Roxanne said, applying antibiotic cream over her work. She stroked his thick hair, pushing back that silver streak that always fell into his eyes. "I'm sorry I kept it from you."

"Why did you?"

"I didn't want to lose you."

"How superficial do you think I am?" He kissed her nose. "You need to understand something. All I ever want is honesty. And your love. You give me that and I won't be going anywhere." He buried his head in her soft hair as she pulled him in for a hug.

"Love?" she said, smiling. "You trying to say you love me?"

"Oh Dr. Roth, I thought I'd made that pretty clear." He kissed her softly on the lips. He stroked her hair, softly at first, and then stronger, as his lips pressed harder. He reached down and put his hand in her panties, touching her lightly.

"Oh god," she said. "Do that. Again."

CHAPTER TWENTY-EIGHT

⌒

Suvir carried a framed photograph of Geeta into the house. During her funeral eulogy it was displayed next to a lit candle. The photograph had been taken in Hawaii two years earlier. Her profile showed her smile, as she watched the humpback whales breach from the balcony suite of their hotel. He stared into the photo after he hung it in its usual spot in the living room, and could almost hear the waves of the ocean and her delighted squeals with each breach.

"It was a lovely ceremony," said a lady he didn't know. Maybe she was someone from Geeta's book club? He thanked her while wondering to himself. They all said variations of the same things to him. "She was such a beautiful lady." "I'm so sorry for your loss." But the worst was, "She's in a better place." He'd heard that for the past week and maybe ten different people had uttered it to him today. It was such a stupid thing to say. To imply that it was better to be dead than to be with him and Anjali. That Geeta didn't want to see her granddaughter be born. They were so stupid. He walked around the lower level of the house, from room to room, its life force vacated. He wanted the strangers to leave him to his misery, to his guilt-ridden, rotten reality.

Someone had placed a buffet of sandwiches on the dining room table. He ate one. It tasted as if air could harden, flavorless and rigid. He forced himself to chew and swallow. He looked around for something to drink and his heart quickened. Rekha, Geeta's twin sister, was on the couch, her arm around Anjali. Rekha didn't have a heart-shaped birthmark above her

"What's your poison?" he said, looking at her figure. Her cleavage was enticing.

"What are my options?"

"It's a thousand dollars for a prescription of oxycodone, morphine, or fentanyl; five hundred dollars for phenteramine and ketamine," he said. "If you prefer, you can pay me by other means."

"I'm not a whore, but there's one in line if you're strapped." She pulled her wallet out. Her manicured nails flipped through the cash of hundreds and she handed him ten bills. "Fentanyl, please."

"No refills." He tore a prescription from the pad.

Homeless addicts carrying plastic bags and cardboard signs, who had no hope of getting a prescription filled by a pharmacy, were in line as well. He "treated" them as well once the housewives were taken care of. They got single pills from prescriptions Seth or Crystal had filled. Fifty dollars a pill. Crystal's cocaine supplier from her strip club kept him well stocked, so D.K. occasionally sold that too, after he'd stepped on it with baking soda.

⌒

In only three weeks, his cocaine and pill mill had amassed over two hundred thousand, tax free, cold hard cash. He spilled bags of it on the floor in the waiting room, a sea of green, and motioned to Crystal.

"Take off just your shirt and lie on it."

Crystal obeyed. "Now take off just your skirt and panties." Crystal wiggled out of her miniskirt and panties, now wearing only a red lace bra. "Damn that's hot." He took several photos of her. He put the phone on video record, propping it up against his shoe on the floor. He'd pinned Crystal's arms above her head and she bit into his shoulder. "Bitch, bite harder!" he said right before he climaxed.

"Maybe not that hard." He laughed, rolling off of her and rubbing his shoulder. Her teeth marks had pierced his skin and it was already bruising.

"I do what you want, and you wanted it," she said, kissing his neck and nuzzling him as he picked up his phone and reviewed the video. "Can I take some of this cash? I'm running low."

D.K. reached to his side and handed her several hundred-dollar bills. "Get some new panties too. I've boned you in all of these already." He sniffed the discarded red panties that were by his head. "Damn your stank turns me on like nothing else."

Well *almost* like nothing else, he thought. He missed cutting on patients. His review board meeting at the hospital was next week, but with all this new cash flow he'd considered blowing it off. But money and sex weren't everything. He missed the thrill of surgery. The slicing of an artery, the severing of a nerve. Nothing could match that high; not cocaine, whores, ketamine. He needed operating room privileges and he needed them stat.

CHAPTER THIRTY

Roxanne was in her twentieth hour of call in labor and delivery, snacking on crackers and peanut butter with the nurses in their lounge. The unit had been relentless; four C-sections and twelve epidurals, and she still had four hours of call left to go. She was grateful for the two nurse anesthetists working with her who were now both off duty.

"I think I might go sleep, too," Roxanne said.

Susan, running her hand through her curly red hair and pinning it back up with a butterfly hair clip, said, "I'm telling you, it's the full moon. There's no point in trying to sleep tonight." Susan had recovered from her seizure without incident.

"You know, statistically, they've shot your theory down."

Wendy poked her head into the lounge. "I'm admitting a direct send from the ER in room six, and they'll need someone soon for an epidural in four."

"Told you," Susan said.

"The theory..." Roxanne wiped the cracker crumbs off her hands and stood. "Is false...except for today."

As Roxanne was getting a history on the pregnant patient in room four, who wasn't yet in active labor, her pager, "the bomb," exploded. It was as startling as a wailing fire truck.

#911-6.

"I'll be back as soon as I can," she told the patient, and bolted out of the room. She stopped abruptly at the sight of a woman pacing in front of room six. She had the same long black hair, almond eyes, and brown skin as Geeta.

"Are you the obstetrician?" the woman said. Her fingers clutched a set of car keys and two purses were slung on her shoulder. "You have to help my niece."

"I'm the anesthesiologist." Roxanne shoved open the door to room six. The woman followed. A young pregnant woman wearing a thin hospital gown was writhing on a stretcher. Her eyes were closed and she was moaning. Roxanne recognized Geeta's daughter and a wave of empathy hit her like a tsunami.

"Thirty-four weeks, breech, one foot's out," Wendy said as she and two other nurses wheeled the stretcher out the door toward the operating room. "We just got her IV in, Dr. Huntington's scrubbing, I hung antibiotics."

"Does she have any medical problems, any allergies?" Roxanne asked the aunt while following behind the stretcher. She put her hair into a cap that she'd pulled out of her back pocket.

"None, but her mother died in the operating room." The aunt's voice sounded like high heels running on concrete. "Oh please, please take care of our Anjali. Please help her. Her husband's on a flight home from Chicago."

"We will," Roxanne called out over her shoulder. "We will."

Any other circumstance of a family death in the operating room would've prompted her to ask about family allergies to anesthesia; specifically the rare genetic disease of malignant hyperthermia, MH. But she knew Geeta didn't die from MH.

Roxanne entered the operating room through the back hallway's narrow corridor and got there before the team rolled the stretcher through the double doors. Dr. Heather Huntington, in scrubs with her long curly blonde hair tucked inside a blue cloth bonnet with the University of Memphis logo on the front, was outside the crash operating room washing her hands at the scrub sink. Susan and a scrub tech were already in the room setting up and preparing the surgical instruments Dr. Huntington would need.

"Heather, do I have time to put in a spinal?" Roxanne said.

"Heart tones down. We need stat general."

At the start of her shift that morning Roxanne had pulled drugs out of the anesthesia cart's medicine tray and drawn them up in syringes, locking the cart behind her. She had also prepared an endotracheal tube.

As she arranged the monitors she looked up as Wendy pushed the stretcher beside the operating table. Anjali, flat on her back, looked around the room and then up at the head of the bed. A flash of recognition crossed her face when she saw Roxanne.

"Oh my god, Dr. Roth, help me. Please help me." Anjali's voice was raised. She clutched Roxanne's like a person drowning. "Don't let my baby die!" Tears streamed down Anjali's face.

"Anjali, I need you to listen to me now honey, okay? We're going to take care of you and your baby, but I need you to help me." She took Anjali's right arm and put it over Anjali's chest. "Put your arms across your chest, Anjali. We're going to move you over to this table." Wendy and Susan placed a metal slab with a black cloth on it under Anjali and quickly transferred her to the operating table.

"Now, a lot's going to happen all at once." Roxanne kept speaking in her slow soothing "Momma Roth" voice. Susan lifted the hospital gown off of Anjali's belly and pressed down on it with a surgical antiseptic to wash her. Roxanne lifted Anjali's arm and placed the blood pressure cuff on. "Anjali, I need to get you under general anesthesia right now, so we can get the baby out."

"No!" Anjali writhed and tried to sit up. "You put my mom to sleep and she never woke!"

The room activity slowed as the OR team looked at Roxanne. Roxanne stroked Anjali's head and bent down to whisper in her ear. "This is nothing like what happened to your mom. I promise you, we don't have a choice right now. I'll be here the whole time and I'll wake you up the second I can, I promise you."

Dr. Huntington and the tech opened the drapes and covered Anjali from her chest down with just her abdomen exposed. Susan and Wendy clamped the sterile drape up on IV poles on either side of the bed by Roxanne.

Roxanne took the oxygen mask and handed it to Wendy. Wendy put in on Anjali's face. As Roxanne pushed drugs through the IV, Anjali continued to wail.

"It's going to be okay, it's going to be okay." Roxanne stroked her head until Anjali went silent. Within fifteen seconds Roxanne had the breathing tube in. She took her stethoscope off from around her neck and listened for breath sounds. Once she heard them, she hollered out, "Cut!"

Dr. Huntington, who was standing with a scalpel in her right hand, placed the metal blade on Anjali's bikini line and made an incision. "We don't know how long the heart tones have been down," Dr. Huntington said, all the while her hands working quickly to expose the uterus. "Is NICU on the way? I need them now. Uterine incision." A gush of meconium poured out of the uterus. "Thick mec, baby's definitely distressed."

Roxanne stood watching over the drapes after turning on the anesthesia gas. Anjali's heart rate was fast but she was otherwise stable. Roxanne prepared a dose of Pitocin. The neonatology nurses arrived.

The team watched as Dr. Huntington maneuvered the baby's head out first, pausing to bulb suction the green fluid off of the baby's nose and mouth before carefully pulling the body out. The baby was blue, not breathing and not crying. Dr. Huntington reached over and handed it to one of the nurses.

Roxanne hung the Pitocin and watched as they resuscitated the baby. They were huddled around her as she lay flaccid on the warming table. They cheered for her as they worked, a melody of "Come on baby, come on little girl, wake up baby girl," as they tapped on her feet and rubbed her head. "Heart rate's ninety." "Suction." A nurse suctioned the baby's mouth and gave her oxygen. "Heart rate's coming up."

A weak little cry.

"Good baby," they cooed and continued to resuscitate her. "Good girl." A moment later a loud and sustained cry. "Atta girl. Get mad at us."

One of the nurses turned to the surgical team. "First Apgar score's four. But now she's looking great. I bet the five-minute will be a nine."

The room's collective relief was almost palpable. Suddenly Anjali's display monitor's tone changed. "Bradycardia," Roxanne said, her voice raised. Anjali's heart, which was beating regularly a moment ago, was now only beating thirty times a minute. Roxanne reached into her drug tray and pushed resuscitation medication through the IV. "Heather, strong vagal response."

"I had just pushed the uterus back in. Shouldn't happen again."

Anjali's heart rate responded to the medicine and was now back to normal. Roxanne gave some narcotics through the IV and began charting while watching over Anjali. When the surgery was over, she turned off the sevo gas and emerged Anjali from anesthesia. Anjali's slow breathing pattern showed the narcotics were working and she opened her eyes when Roxanne told her to. Roxanne pulled the tube.

"All done, Anjali. You have a beautiful baby girl," Roxanne said, while stroking her hair. "Congratulations." Anjali blinked. Her mouth formed a smile.

"Meet your daughter," the NICU nurse said, presenting the baby to Anjali. The baby's eyes were closed and she was swaddled in a warm pink hospital baby blanket. They had also put a pink cap on her. Anjali cried and laughed at the same time. She cradled the baby on her chest while the nurse helped hold her for support.

"Hi there, Marie Geeta Anjali. I'm your mommy." She kissed the baby's forehead, her tears wetting the baby's cheeks.

"I'm going to carry the baby for you until you can sit up in bed, okay?" The nurse said. She pulled the pink cap off the baby for a moment. "She's beautiful, look at all that gorgeous hair on her."

Anjali released the baby to her. She tilted her head up to look for Roxanne. When she saw her, she reached up and grasped Roxanne's hand. "Dr. Roth, thank you."

"You did so great." She paused and stroked Anjali's hair out of her eyes. "I'm sure your mother would be honored by the name."

"We'll call her Marie. That was my grandmother's middle name…three generations in one little baby." Tears flowed from Anjali's eyes. "But I'm the only one of us she'll know."

Roxanne fought back tears of her own.

CHAPTER THIRTY-ONE

⌒

"I can't do it," Roxanne said and folded her arms on the dining table to bury her head. "I couldn't save her. These books are useless." It was ten o'clock on a Saturday night. Her table was littered with Justin's surgical textbooks competing for room with her anesthesiology oral board review material. A four-inch binder, called "Big Red," was open in front of Justin. He was in the middle of giving her a mock exam.

"Come on. Just answer this last question for me. Why be concerned about placing a central line in a patient with a left bundle branch block?"

"It can cause complete heart block."

"Very good, babe." He reached across the table and stroked her head. "Stop blaming yourself, there's nothing else you could've done for Geeta."

"I should have refused to put her to sleep. I should've just cancelled it." She propped her chin in her hands. "My job was to protect her, and I didn't. Ask the examiners, they'll tell you I'm right."

"You have to stop beating yourself up. The system failed her. But you need to practice for this exam."

"I can't. I just can't. I'll try tomorrow. Can we stop?"

"Trolley ride?" Justin put the highlighter down. "Get you some fresh air."

Justin took a bottle of beer out of the fridge and tucked it into his winter coat pocket. They boarded the river loop trolley to South Main Street. A Garth Brooks concert had just let out of the FedEx Forum and the street was full of pedestrians, wearing cowboy boots and hats, and speed walking to get out of the cold.

"The medical board still hasn't responded to my complaint about D.K. I got only the form letter standard reply that they will look into the matter, but it's been a month and nothing."

Justin turned to her from the window. "Let's call them again, Monday? The med ex committee's meeting is when? In two weeks? Armstrong said both of us should come." He took a sip from the bottle of beer he'd snuck on. "They won't give him privileges."

"But he needs his license revoked or he'll just go work at another hospital." She took out her phone and looked at the calendar. "Med exec's in three weeks, on February 27. I'm going to voice record the whole thing and send the state medical board a detailed transcript of everything we know he's done. I don't care if it's illegal."

Roxanne noticed four people standing single file on the side of an office building. Memphis Neurosurgical read the bold blue sign above the entrance and the lights were off inside. "What's going on down there, you think?" She pointed. "Why would anybody be at D.K.'s office this late?"

"Only one way to find out." Justin stood and pulled the lever for the next stop. When they got off the trolley, he took her gloved hand in his and walked toward the office building.

They approached the last person in line, a twenty-something kid, his right arm amputated. His sweatshirt hadn't seen a washer in months and he had holes in his shoes. His dog, flea bitten and with mange, was sitting by his side. The kid carried a tattered cardboard sign under his bad arm that read Homeless, Hungry, Please Help.

"Why're you in line to see a neurosurgeon?" Roxanne said. "At this hour?"

"You a cop?"

"No, we aren't cops. We're in…finance." She reached into her purse, pulled out a twenty-dollar bill, and handed it to him. "What're you in line for?"

He took the twenty and put it in his front jean pocket. "Okay…but you didn't hear it from me, got it?"

"Okay."

"He's got everything in there. You hand him cash and he'll give you pills on the spot." He glanced behind him. It was dark and he was speaking so softly no one else could hear him, but he lowered his voice anyway. "Fentanyl, morphine, special K. He's got it all, lady. I just do pills now." He held up his stump. "Can't shoot up no more. Got bad infected from a dirty needle, they cut it off to save my life."

Justin leaned in closer to the kid. "So the doctor in there will give me pills? I just have to give him cash?"

"Yup." The kid nodded vigorously. "Name's Webb. Dude, he's the plug. He'll get you lit."

The trolley was approaching and Justin took Roxanne by the hand, pulling her toward the trolley stop. "Thanks, man." Justin waved at him. "Our ride's here."

The trolley was crowded with loud concert goers and they found a bench in the sea of cowboy hats. Roxanne shook her head in astonishment. "He doesn't just *do* drugs, he *deals* drugs."

Justin pulled out his smartphone and showed it to Roxanne. The voice recorder was still on. He pushed *stop, play* and raised the volume to maximum. The kid's voice was soft but clear, the entire conversation recorded. "Fentanyl, morphine, special K. He's got it all lady. I just do pills now." Justin fast-forwarded. "Name's Webb."

"Holy shit."

"I did what you were going to do at the meeting. We needed more ammo and now we have it."

Roxanne showered him with kisses on his cheeks and his forehead. "Okay, so what should we do first? How do we handle this? Let's call the police. They'll go arrest him."

"I think we go to the DEA...they would be the ones to do a drug bust. They would get warrants and do it correctly. The cops would just bust up the party tonight. I don't know if they could even enter without warrants."

"Yeah and what if he just didn't answer the door? He could hide it all and get away with it."

"Exactly."

"Okay." Roxanne took off her right glove and used Google search to find a number. "Calling the DEA."

It went straight to voicemail. She rolled her eyes and whispered into the phone. "This is Dr. Roxanne Roth. I am calling to report a pill mill being run out of Dr. D.K. Webb's office in Memphis, Tennessee. Please call me back." She repeated her phone number twice and then hung up.

"Dickie, you murderer, we're putting you in jail." She took a long swig of Justin's beer before kissing him.

CHAPTER THIRTY-TWO

———

"Dr. Webb, reporting for duty," D.K. said. He placed his motorcycle helmet on the secretary's desk and shook his bike jacket off his six-foot-four frame. By speeding on the freeway over the Hernando de Soto Bridge, it had taken him only forty-five minutes to get to Memorial Hospital in Arkansas from his downtown apartment. He'd weaved around the Mac trucks and cars with a combination of ecstasy and cocaine pumping through his veins.

A woman in surgical attire with her hair in a cap bounded from her seat at the OR control desk. "We've been expecting you. Let me show you around. I'm Natalie. I'll be circulating in your room." She walked out of the booth and shut the door behind her. D.K. studied her. He thought about how perfect her ass was in those tight white scrubs.

"You'll be in OR four, we only have five, it's down the hall on the left. The scrub tech pulled all the instruments you requested." She scanned her badge on the door's reader. "Pre-op and recovery share the same space. Your patient's been ready for an hour; he drove in from Memphis too. That's quite a haul to have surgery, no?"

"Yeah, they didn't have any openings for him in Memphis, but you could...fit me in." D.K. put the helmet under his right arm. "He's in a lot of pain. I didn't want him to wait. Believe me, I'd rather work locally too."

"Well, I'm glad we could accommodate you."

"Speaking of?" His gaze upon her body was intrusive as he rubbed his cheek. His beard was scruffy, as he hadn't shaved or showered since yesterday morning.

Natalie's mouth lost the smile. "You can stop ogling me." She held up a diamond ring on her left hand. "The men's locker room's right through that door. There should be scrubs in the cubbies. I'll page the anesthesiologist to let him know you're here."

He watched her walk away. She just needed some persuasion; it was clear from her choice of uniform she wanted attention. The locker room was as cramped as an airplane and smelled of man sweat. This really is a shitty hospital, he thought. He deserved a state-of-the-art facility with wide hallways and the newest equipment, not this rat hole. But it would do, he could operate anywhere and with any tools. He changed into extra-large green scrubs and caught his reflection as he tied on his surgical cap. His eyes were bloodshot. He pulled some Visine out of his bike jacket and dropped it in his eyes. He looked in the mirror again. That's better, he thought; no one could resist those baby blues.

He dropped a tablet under his tongue and enjoyed the sensation surging through his brain. He started to smack his lips and reached into his pocket for some gum to mask the effects of ecstasy.

His patient, Dr. Edward Stewart, was a sonar engineer. He'd developed successful technology, had it patented, which led to millions and an early retirement. He told D.K. in his office last month, "Retirement would be a lot more fun if I could play golf. This damn back of mine won't let me swing." He'd already consulted two neurosurgeons who'd reviewed his MRI but told him an operation wouldn't help him.

"They don't see what I see." D.K. had pointed to a normal lumbar spine on the MRI image and explained. "This right here should have more room. It's compressed just enough that other docs don't see it, but it's right there and causing you pain. If I take the disc out, it'll alleviate the pressure and you'll have immediate relief. In before breakfast, out by dinnertime."

"The exact words I needed to hear, doc. Tell me when and where and I'm there."

D.K. entered pre-op and found his patient. "You ready to roll?" he said, extending his right hand. D.K. chewed his gum.

"Yes sir. When I said when and where I didn't think you meant Arkansas." He laughed.

"Sorry for the drive, Memphis is just too busy. I knew you would prefer to get it done."

"You got that right."

"You want to live well, not just live." He smiled. "Okay then, I'll see you when you wake up. They'll get you back there and off to sleep."

Natalie was waiting at the desk. She pushed the stretcher down the hall to the operating room while he watched her; his gaze glued on her every step, watching her generous backside rock back and forth.

⌒

Something was terribly wrong, Natalie thought. She was standing at the head of the bed by the anesthesiologist, Kevin Johnson, and they looked over the drape together. Blood was pouring from the open wound in Edward Stewart's back. She'd never seen it happen on a lumbar disc.

"What's going on, where's the bleeding from?" she whispered to Dr. Johnson.

"He's not answering me." He spoke loudly. "Dr. Webb? Do you need assistance?"

The surgeon peered into the microscope lens that was draped sterilely over the patient.

"Hey!" Dr. Johnson's voice louder. "Hey! Webb? Are you there?"

The surgeon remained silent.

"Call stat for security and Dr. Starling. I think we have an imposter here," Dr. Johnson said. "I need any surgeon available now. Call a code if you have to." He reached into his drug tray and spiked resuscitation drugs. The patient didn't need them yet but he would soon if this stranger with the scalpel didn't stop the bloodletting.

"I hear you, dude," D.K. said. "It's fine. I can handle this pumper. Was just watching it for a second." D.K. held a suction tip to the bleed and cleared blood from the field. It continued to pour out from the wound.

Dr. Johnson said to Natalie, "Get Dr. Starling. Now!"

Natalie sprinted out of the operating room to the control desk. She told the unit secretary, "We've got a situation in four. Call security, call a code, and I need Dr. Starling's number. Quick." She grabbed the printed directory of staff off the wall, dialed the number on the portable phone, and ran back to the operating room.

When she got there, she saw the two-liter suction canister was now full of bright blood. The surgeon continued to peer into the microscope and suction all the while shifting left and right on his heels.

Dr. Johnson had spiked a bag of epinephrine. "Natalie, get four units Type O neg in here," he said.

"Dr. Starling, we need you right now in room four," Natalie said into the phone while nodding at the anesthesiologist. "Stat, yes. I can't talk." She hung up and called the blood bank. "We need four units stat on Edward Stewart, FIN 0286168. I know he's not type and crossed, send O negative, it's an emergency."

"Relax, Arkansas piglets," D.K. said. "I've got it under control."

A petite woman of Chinese descent entered wearing a bunny suit over her slacks and blouse; her short black hair pulled into a disposable blue bonnet. "I raced from the downstairs clinic. What's going on?" She tied her scrub mask on.

"Who are you?" D.K.'s pupils were dilated and sweat poured from his forehead. He smacked his gum behind his bloodied sterile mask.

"Dr. Starling, Chief of Neurosurgery, I'm scrubbing in. I need 6.5 gloves," she said to the scrub tech.

"Well get out of my operating room, *Darling*," he said. "I don't need your help."

"It's *Starling* and I beg to differ." She walked out to scrub her hands at the sink.

The code team, five nurses, and an internal medical doctor, all dressed like Dr. Starling in white sterile zip ups, entered the OR with a drug cart. The anesthesiologist was placing another IV in the left wrist.

"I can't place a central line with the patient prone," he said. "I've never needed a central line on a damn disc. Someone get me another IV on the right hand and someone spike more blood. I need a cardiac drug box. I need an art line set up. Get me a type and cross pink top."

"Would you please calm the hell down?" D.K. said. He glanced at the head of the bed and continued to peer into the microscope, his hands still.

While the code team worked, Dr. Starling, now gowned and gloved, went on the opposite side of the operating bed from D.K. and looked through the microscope lens the tech had been using. Her eyes widened.

"You're way too deep and lateral, I think you've cut into the iliac artery. I've never seen…" she said. She turned to Dr. Johnson. "We need to go supine stat to open the abdomen and stop the bleed. There's no way to stop it prone. Natalie, call vascular or cardiothoracic. We need general, too." The code team assisted Natalie with the string of orders. They opened supplies for the tech and dumped them sterilely onto her surgical table.

"But we don't have cardiothoracic here anymore. Our only vascular doctor is out of town," Natalie said. "She left for a conference yesterday."

"Are you all deaf?" D.K. said. "I can stop the bleed, I see it."

"No you can't, there's even more blood in the abdomen. You can't clamp it or put pressure from here. And you're obviously impaired, whoever you are." She saw the security guard walk in and pointed to D.K. "Get this guy out of here. He's murdering a patient."

"I told you this is my case." D.K. hovered his scalpel over Dr. Starling's hands as if to slice her. Dr. Starling hopped back, jerking both of her hands away.

The tech pulled the tray of instruments away from D.K. and when he turned to grab the suction from her the security guard jumped him from behind.

"Hey!" D.K. said.

"You move and I'll break your wrists," the guard said, even though D.K. had the height and weight advantage. He held D.K.'s arms in a vise tightly behind his head. Dr. Johnson kicked D.K.'s legs out from under him so he fell to the floor.

"Lie the hell down," Dr. Johnson said with his foot on D.K.'s back. The guard dragged D.K. to the door, where another guard had arrived to cuff him.

"Do you know who you're messing with?" D.K. said as the guards pushed him out of the room. "You're all out of your league, I'm the only one that can save the patient."

"Shut up," the guard said. "Or I really will break your wrists."

Dr. Starling sewed as fast as she could to close the posterior wound so they could turn the patient onto his back. "Take out the scope," she said. "Let's go supine. Call med evac and tell The Med we're coming. Natalie, get me a general surgeon. We have to open the abdomen and clamp the aorta but we'll need a vascular team to repair." She looked up at the head of the bed. "How's the pressure, Kevin?"

"Epi wide open, six units in, crossmatched blood on the way. But he's spiraling." The anesthesiologist shook his head. "I don't think we can get him to Memphis."

They turned him from his belly onto a stretcher. His face was up now. Dr. Johnson held the breathing tube in place as they returned him to the operating room table. They prepped him with Betadine but as Dr. Starling cut into his abdomen to explore for the internal bleed, his heart beat for the last time.

They coded him for thirty minutes before Dr. Johnson said, "I'm calling it." The code team stopped doing chest compressions. Dr. Starling stepped away from the table.

"Time of death, thirteen thirty-one. Cause of death, a psychopath surgeon from Memphis, Tennessee," Dr. Johnson said and tore his mask off.

CHAPTER THIRTY-THREE

⌒

"I get a lawyer," D.K. told the intake officer, a muscular white man with silver hair. D.K. stood looking around the concrete walls, his hands still cuffed behind him. He needed to rub his nose. "Get these handcuffs off me. Do you people know who I am?"

"All right, son. Pipe down." The officer wore a short-sleeve shirt with an Arkansas Department of Corrections badge on his left sleeve. He had a walkie talkie on his hip, the microphone clipped near his left shoulder. "I know who you are. Do you know who *I* am is the question." He made a sweeping gesture with his right hand, the small room filled only with his desk and two uncomfortable metal chairs. "I'm Deputy Brennan and this is intake." A large window reinforced with safety glass was behind him, as were his fellow deputies behind the glass. "We don't get doctors around here much. You want to tell me what happened?"

"Your men arrested me for nothing, is what," D.K. said. "Now please uncuff me. I know my rights."

"They tell me you assaulted another doctor with a scalpel."

"And I'm telling you I want my lawyer."

"You'll get one." He went around to the front of his desk. "I need to frisk you first. Spread your legs." The deputy patted down D.K.'s legs and waist. "I'm going to lift your shirt up."

D.K. held still for him.

"I need some water," D.K. said. He had a pounding headache and was sweating profusely.

"Soon," the deputy said, satisfied with the frisk. "I'm going to uncuff you big guy, but you need to keep your hands behind you at all times." He tilted his head to the double-pane windows. "They're watching." He walked back around his desk and got a set of keys from a drawer. He unlocked the handcuffs.

D.K. massaged his wrists. "These are worth millions, you better be glad they didn't get hurt."

"Uh-huh. Keep 'em behind you if you want to it to stay that way."

The deputy sat at his desk and pointed for D.K. to sit across from him. He logged into his computer and began to itemize the belongings in the personal property bag; wallet, bike helmet, keys, Swiss Army knife. He opened the pockets of the jacket and a small bag of white powder fell out. He opened it and sniffed.

"That's medicinal," D.K said. "I use it on patients to close the wound in the OR. It vasoconstricts and stops the bleeding." His head felt like hammers were pressing against both temples, the throbbing pain worsening. He needed that vasoconstriction right now in his cranial vessels.

"Uh huh." The deputy typed into the computer. "Pretty sure that's bullshit, sir." He reached in a desk drawer and pulled out an inkless scanner with a green light. "Put four fingers here, not your thumb yet. Right hand first."

"They fingerprinted me for my medical licenses," he said. "Is this necessary?"

"As necessary as your booking photo."

"A mug shot?"

"Maybe you should look around." The deputy waved his arms around him, palms up. "This is jail. We read your rights. I believe you should remember the procedure, *three* juvi arrests, was it?"

"How'd you know about those?"

"Only cleared from public record, not ours." He tapped his computer and then tapped the fingerprint scanner. "Right hand first." He motioned again for D.K. to place his hand on it. D.K. obeyed and the deputy continued. "The prosecutor will decide what charges to file, if any. You'll have an arraignment, where you can have a lawyer present. District Court of St. Francis County is held Monday, Wednesday, and Thursday at 1:00 p.m."

"Not until Wednesday?" D.K. felt himself starting to shake and couldn't control the tremors in his hand. He couldn't stay in jail for two days. He would go through withdrawal; he couldn't do that on the concrete floor of a jail cell like some scumbag.

"You're here until the arraignment. Could be Wednesday, could be next week."

"You're going to have to put me in medical. I've got a seizure disorder. I'll seize without medicine."

"I see." The deputy reached into a file cabinet behind him, pulled out a form, and placed it in front of D.K. with a pen. "Fill out this inmate sick care request, list the medication you need."

D.K. stared at the page, and then began to write, his penmanship uneven as his hand continued to tremble. One drug, propranolol would lower his heart rate and blood pressure and the other, diazepam, would curb his anxiety. He handed it back to the deputy. "I take both, twice a day."

"I'll get it to the medical staff." He punched some numbers into a fax machine and sent the form. "Now I'll take that photo and show you to holding. You'll be there until the arraignment."

"You can't leave me in a cell. I'll seize and die. Do you want that on your record?"

"It's just a holding room. And we'll get you your medicine, they're surprisingly efficient in medical. Now come on, this way, you can make your phone call." He stood and opened the wood door. "After you. Continue to keep your hands behind you."

He was taken to a larger room with concrete walls and bright fluorescent lighting.

Four payphones were hanging on the wall, one occupied by a crying teenage girl in ripped jeans and no shoes. "I didn't do it, Mom, I swear," she cried into the phone. "Please come get me."

He chose the phone on the opposite end, picked it up, and heard a dial tone. The Deputy handed him a token and said, "It's the only one you get, so choose wisely. You've got five minutes."

He knew Crystal's number from memory. She and Seth were the only two people he trusted, anyway. He was their general and they were good soldiers, as long as he supplied the cash and drugs. He put the phone back in the cradle. "Will you bring me some water?" When he wiped the sweat off his forehead with his sleeve, his scrubs smelled of dried blood.

The deputy pointed to the water fountain at the end of the hall. "Go drink."

D.K. lapped at the water. That damn deputy was going to listen to his call, he thought. He hoped Crystal would remember their code words. He'd recently updated an escape plan if needed but he needed her to do her part. She knew what to do *if* she wasn't high.

She answered.

"It's me," he said. "We've got three medals, right now."

"What? Three? Medal what?"

"Crystal. Remember on the patio that day? We discussed this?" He tapped his fingers on the top of the payphone, leaned over, and took a deep breath. "Three damn medals."

"Shit! Now I remember."

"Forrest City, Arkansas."

"I'll call Frank. I'll arrange everything, everything. Don't you worry, baby. I got this."

"I'm counting on you." He hung up the phone. He just had to endure until Wednesday.

"You'll wait in our bullpen," Deputy Brennan said. "All the solitary rooms are full." He led D.K. to a room with six plastic chairs and four cots on the floor. There was a metal toilet in the corner and the room smelled like urine. A pit bull of a man, wearing no shoes or shirt, was passed out on a cot, his torn jeans with a stain in the crotch.

"I'm not going in here, are you nuts?" D.K. said.

"I'm sorry our bed and breakfast isn't up to your standards, doctor," the deputy said. He pushed him inside and locked the metal bars behind him. "It's just two days, right?"

D.K. walked around the urine stains on the concrete floor, circling the cell. He felt as if ants were crawling on him. He wasn't sure if it was withdrawal or actual ants and lifted his shirt to examine his skin. Nothing was there.

"I need my medicine," he called out to the empty corridor. He gripped the bars of the door. "I'll seize soon." D.K. didn't know how much time passed, but it felt like hours before the deputy returned.

"Here you go," he said. Through the bars, he handed D.K. water in a paper cup and two pills. "As you requested."

"Can I get some food?" D.K. gulped the pills down. "It's supposed to be taken on a full stomach."

"Dinner tray is at 18:00."

D.K. pointed to the man still asleep on the floor. "And how am I supposed to deal with that when it wakes up?"

"Not feeling so brave without your scalpel?"

"I don't want to have to hurt that beast is all," D.K. said. "Can I have a solitary room?"

"I'll let you know if there's a vacancy." The deputy chuckled and walked away.

⌒

Once the medicine kicked in, D.K. began to feel calm. He sat on the cot furthest from the man, and propped himself up against the concrete wall. Over the next thirty-six hours, two other men were placed in the room. He called one of them "Chatty Cathy" and told him to shut up every few hours. The men left him alone.

He ate the trays of stale bread and rubbery chicken, dozing on and off until he was escorted to the courthouse. He'd never been more relieved to see a bathroom.

And then his goddess Crystal showed up. She'd worn her most conservative outfit to the arraignment, a tweed miniskirt with a black lace fitted top and a matching tweed blazer that she didn't button. Her shoes, red high heels, and her usual false eyelashes and eye glitter, completed the look. He gave her a hug and nuzzled her. She was now his everything.

"Put this on." She spoke into his ear and handed him a suit. "Three medals is a go."

CHAPTER THIRTY-FOUR

After the arraignment, D.K. and Crystal walked into the corridor of the courthouse with Frank Lipman, attorney at law. One family, flanked by several lawyers, mingled in the corner of the room with high ceilings and unobstructed floor space. The men's gazes landed on Crystal as her heels tapped on the laminate floor.

"Wait," Frank told D.K. and Crystal as they headed to the exit. He opened the courthouse door, but then quickly closed it. "I was afraid of this. There's a Memphis news truck," Frank said. "Parked right out front. Vultures drove to Arkansas to cover an arrested doctor." Frank popped his head out squinting his eyes, his white bald head reflected in the sunlight. He pulled back inside and tightened his coat around him. "It's the 5:00 team," he said. "We'll have three hours before it hits. I'll pull my car up and you just get in. Do not look at the camera, do not acknowledge the reporter. And put on your sunglasses."

"Judge released me, man." D.K. kept his sunglasses on the top of his head. He wore the suit Crystal had brought him, his bloodied scrubs in the bathroom garbage. He carried his plastic personal property bag.

"She released you on $100,000 bail," Frank said. "But the hospital's assault charges stand. The only reason you're out is because I convinced her you're not a flight risk." He took the plastic bag from him. "Are you? A flight risk?"

"He's got me to look after," Crystal said, wrapping her hand around D.K.'s bicep. "He's not going anywhere."

"That's right." D.K. patted Crystal's arm. "And the judge cancelled my passport, man, I can't go anywhere." He was exhausted from sleeping on the thin mat, the only thing between him and a concrete floor. He smelled like the floor too. Being locked up had given him the courage he needed to solidify his plan.

"Crystal, I want you to come with me," Frank said. "This is Forrest City. They don't need to see you two…together."

"What's that supposed to mean?" she said. "What's wrong with being seen with me?"

"You think this town is named for trees?" said Frank. "It's named for Nathan Bedford Forrest, the first head wizard of the KKK. Trust me on this and come on." He held the door open for her.

"Fine, I'll walk without my man, but I ain't scared of the KKK or anyone else," she said.

"Dr. Webb, I'll text you when we're out front. I'm in a black Lexus 350." He looked back at D.K. and said, "Say nothing to the press."

D.K. paced alone in the courthouse. He was jonesing for a hit and ready to get back to his stash. He looked out the window. A douche bag reporter was standing on the sidewalk in front of a camera. D.K. watched as he fixed his hair and tested his microphone. He wanted to punch him.

D.K. scrolled through his smartphone and read the *Drudge Report* online. The president's latest allegation that the FBI wiretapped him cracked him up. That guy could do or say anything and no one could touch him. Just like me, he thought. Just like me. He got the text from Frank, flipped his sunglasses on, and strode outside, ignoring the news team as instructed.

Frank drove them to Memphis Neurosurgical and they entered the back entrance just in case there were news crews out front. D.K. reached across the passenger seat and shook Frank's hand firmly. "Thanks for everything. You'll tell me when the trial date gets set?"

"Lay low for now, okay? Close the clinic and stay out of trouble. I'll be in touch."

"You got it," he said and got out. He held the rear door open for Crystal and offered her his hand. They went into the clinic and locked the door.

"We've got to move fast babe, I'm not doing another damn second of jail time," he said. He pulled out two suitcases from the hall closet and handed one to her. "Pack summer clothes for us and all the prescription bottles we have in here. I'll pack this one. Seth knows?"

They heard a knock on the back door and she looked through the peephole. "That's him now," she said.

"You did good, babe," D.K. said. He went to his office, opened a cabinet and punched in the four numbers to his safe. He immediately took a hit of the cocaine he found inside before pocketing two fake passports and visas. He'd had Crystal's passport made months ago; he would never leave her behind as a loose end. She'd confess at the first threat of complicity. He counted all fifty of the prepaid credit cards, totaling fifty thousand dollars. Not every business took cash, and he figured the airlines would flag a cash purchase these days.

He wasn't going to leave Crystal behind, but Seth he could trust. Seth was his bro. He handed him the suitcase he'd filled with cash, cocaine, ketamine, and fentanyl. "Dude. Sell off the rest of the drugs as fast as you can. Keep ten percent for yourself." He handed him an envelope. "Wire the cash. The details are here." D.K. reached into his motorcycle jacket and threw him a set of keys. "My bike's in the hospital parking lot in Arkansas, if they didn't impound it yet. Get it and sell it, too. Fast."

Seth caught the keys. "Will do. Anything else?"

"Can you drop us at the airport in a few?"

"Yeah man, of course. No problem."

After D.K. showered the stench of urine off, brushed his teeth, shaved, and changed into jeans and a T-shirt, he felt like himself. He helped Crystal close the suitcase, which was filled with their clothes and prescription bottles, as he'd instructed. "Too many." D.K. took twenty bottles out, put them in a garbage bag, and handed them to Seth. "Sell these, too."

He zipped the suitcase and looked around the clinic one last time as he put his biker coat back on. "Clean this place out, sell everything you can." He looked at his Rolex. "Let's get the hell out of here, news hits in an hour."

CHAPTER THIRTY-FIVE

Roxanne felt a paw pushing on her leg and reached down to pet Lyla. "Okay baby, we're going, we're going." She leashed Lyla. Justin was putting on his leather coat. "Ready?"

Justin handed her the fuchsia jacket. "You'll be cold, the sun's going down."

She put it on. It was nice to have someone care again if she was warm or not. Holding hands, they walked Lyla and Wrigley through the park and down South Main Street. The Memphis foliage was confused by all the erratic weather they'd had; some tulips were blooming, while others had bloomed too soon and died of frostbite.

They passed a bar with open doors, the TVs blaring behind patrons drinking beer. Plates with names of patrons who'd tasted two hundred of the beers they served hung on the walls and ceiling. "Saucers of Cirrhosis," Justin called it. Roxanne glanced up at the TV and stopped walking abruptly. She pulled on Justin's hand and leaned in closer to the bar window to see. Justin turned back to look at her and followed her gaze to the TV mounted above the bar. They couldn't hear over the loud music but they could read the large caption scrolling underneath.

A local news reporter was standing outside of a jail she didn't recognize in broad daylight. It definitely wasn't Memphis; that jail was on the outskirts of downtown and easily identifiable. What had caught her eye was a flash of platinum blonde hair on a tall man she instantly recognized. D.K., wearing a motorcycle jacket and sunglasses and entering a black SUV, had the reporter's microphone shoved in his face. D.K. pushed it away and shut the door. He disappeared behind the tinted windows of the SUV. Justin and Roxanne watched, stunned, as the video showed the vehicle drive away.

The reporter turned to address the audience. The jail was visible again behind him. They read the captioned dialogue at the bottom of the screen.

"That was him, Memphis Neurosurgeon Dr. D.K. Webb, who has just posted $100,000 bond after spending two nights at this jail, in Forrest City, Arkansas. The doctor was arrested on two charges of aggravated assault with a deadly weapon, and possession of a controlled substance. Sources inside the local hospital tell us a man died Monday due to a botched surgery by Dr. Webb. Dr. Webb's trial date is pending. We at WMTV5, where local news comes first, will keep you posted as details emerge. Back to you, David."

"He went to Arkansas," Roxanne said. "I knew he would find somewhere else to cut. He has a damn Arkansas license."

"And Arkansas let him go," Justin said, tugging gently on Wrigley's leash as the beagle tried to enter the bar. "He'll skip out."

"All his stuff's here, his office, his drug scene. He won't just leave?"

"Drugs are everywhere."

"But don't they take your passports when you get arrested? He can't get that far."

"Babe, that man won't be at his court date."

Roxanne shook her head. "Ran a pill mill, killed two patients that we know of, maimed who knows how many others…and he's out free." The sun was setting as they started their walk back home, hand in hand. "He could stand in the middle of South Main Street, shoot someone, and still get away with it." The anger inside Roxanne felt like a hurricane brewing for weeks was about to hit the shore. "No. He's not getting away."

She pulled on Lyla's leash and tugged Justin's arm, turning them in the opposite direction. "I want to confront that bastard."

"Where?"

"His office. We're calling the police. To hell with warrants."

When they arrived, they saw the lights in front were off. News teams were milling around at the curb. They walked to the back of the building and peered through the windows. No one was there.

CHAPTER THIRTY-SIX

～

The main terminal of the Memphis airport was nearly devoid of passengers as D.K. and Crystal bounded in. When Delta Airlines moved its hub to Atlanta the void it created in Memphis was significant; it was early afternoon but D.K. saw on the entrance monitors there were only eight flights left to depart. He was determined to get on one of them. "Follow me," he said, as he walked to the priority line of Delta's check in. He turned his gaze to the airline agent, a woman with porcelain white skin wearing a red bow around her neck in a navy blue uniform with crisply ironed white lapels on her shirt. She smiled as she typed into her computer.

"Two for Rio? *Today*?" she said, her red bow bobbing up and down with her head.

"Yes, Ma'am," D.K. said, "My gorgeous fiancé is dancing in Carnival." He spun Crystal around in her tweed suit. "She's going to be one of the samba queens at a finale. You should see this goddess is her outfit."

The agent smiled but kept her eyes on the screen. "I've got two seats left on the next flight. It leaves in forty minutes so we have to hurry. You'll have a tight fifty-minute connection in Atlanta then direct to Rio. You'll have to move fast from the domestic terminal to international, but it's easy to do on the tram." She frowned. "Slight problem, all the coach seats are booked. I've only got first class available. I can search tomorrow's flights."

D.K. smiled, pushed his sunglasses on top of his head, his platinum hair held back, and flashed a grin. He leaned forward and whispered. "It's not a problem, we prefer first class." He made a point of glancing at his Rolex as he handed her the passports and a Visa card.

"Looks like your visas for Brazil are up to date as well, Mr. Conway," she said, typing their passport details into the computer. "They are good for ninety days, so when is your return date?"

"I don't know actually, Jenn, what do you think?" He glanced at Crystal.

"Maybe we can take some side trips after? Let's book one-way and decide later."

"Okay. One-way then, all set." The agent finished typing. "Let's hurry and get the bags checked while we still have time. How many?"

"Just this one," D.K. said, lifting it onto the conveyor scale by the agent's computer.

She handed him the boarding passes, and showed him the baggage claim sticker on the back of his. "Have fun at Carnival. TSA's to your right. Don't dawdle, we'll be boarding first class in ten minutes."

D.K. put his arm around Crystal's shoulder and kissed her on the cheek as they walked to security. He whispered in her ear. "Don't worry babe, that travel ban doesn't apply to us. They don't care who's *leaving* the country."

She wrapped her arm around him and said, "I don't worry when I'm with you."

The security line was short, as was the TSA agent surveying them: a thin man with his TSA gold badge above his left breast pocket. He furrowed his brow as he glanced at the passports. "Rio?"

"We're headed to Carnival. My beautiful baby wants to dance." D.K. kissed Crystal's cheek. "Isn't she incredible?"

The agent was silent but took a thorough look at Crystal before studying the passports. He scanned each one. The scanner made a loud beep each time. He handed the passports back to them.

"Next," he said and waved for the next traveler to come forward.

D.K. and Crystal proceeded through the metal detectors. D.K. knew better than to carry his knife and had packed it in his checked bag. "We're going to have to bolt to get down to B20 in time, you ready?" He took her carry-on from her and they bounded past the shops. The smell of BBQ permeated the air. All of a sudden, every TV monitor, which displayed the same station at every gate, blasted a video of him leaving jail.

"Damn," he whispered to Crystal, looking at the TV. He put his sunglasses back on and reached into his backpack. He pulled out a black baseball cap and tucked his hair in. "Just keep walking."

They were the last to board the plane, and were seated in the second row of first class. "Can I bring you a beverage?" the flight attendant said. "We have just a few minutes."

"Yes ma'am, can I please have a martini, dirty if you have it. She'll have a white wine." He held Crystal's hand. They were already five minutes delayed.

Minutes ticked away. He tried to read the *Wall Street Journal* the attendant had brought with the martini; Crystal listened to music on her smartphone through headphones. She rummaged through her purse and pulled out two Percocet, handed one to D.K., and took the other with the last sip of her wine.

A voice came on the overhead. "Welcome passengers, this is First Captain Matthew Coffey. We're currently second in line for take-off and are expected to be in the air in approximately seven minutes. We have a forty-five-minute flight time but I will try to make up some time in the air to help with all those tight connections. I'll talk to you again before we reach Atlanta. Flight attendants, prepare the cabin for take-off."

D.K. swallowed the Percocet, his knee restless. Crystal squeezed his knee to calm him. He stared out the window and leaned back when they finally took off. The sun had just set and the horizon had a pink glow, the sky above them darkening. He took Crystal's hand and put it on the bulge in his trousers. She smiled as her long acrylic nails gently stroked him over his jeans. He put the newspaper over her hand and closed his eyes for a few minutes. He was glad he'd brought her; she might only be with him for money but no one could soothe him like she could.

D.K. scrolled through his phone and copied down a few phone numbers onto a yellow paper note then tucked it in his wallet. "Give me your phone, too," he said to Crystal.

She unplugged her headphones and handed it to him. "You'll buy me a new one?"

"I'll buy whatever you want."

He turned their phones off and put them in his coat pocket. When the plane reached the gate in Atlanta, he and Crystal were the first to stand. He grabbed her belongings from the overhead bin and whispered in her ear, "Fly like the wind, babe. We have eight minutes."

As they maneuvered through the heavy pedestrian traffic in the B terminal, D.K. tossed both of their cell phones into one of the automatic trash compactors. They ran down the escalator and squeezed into the crowded tram as the doors were closing.

It took three minutes to get to the international terminal. D.K. led, and as they ran up the escalator, with him jostling people out of their way, Crystal's red heel got stuck in the grate. "Problem," she called out to D.K. who was already at the top. She wiggled her foot and tried to free the heel but couldn't.

"Women," D.K. said to the travelers standing in front of Crystal, as he went against traffic back down the escalator toward her. He unstrapped her ankle, lifted her foot out of the shoe, and left the shoe in the grate. It caused the escalator to screech to a stop when it hit the top. "Leave it," D.K. said. "I'll buy you better ones."

Crystal took off her other shoe and ran barefoot. They made it to their gate but the Delta agent was closing the jet bridge door.

"Wait!" D.K. said sprinting. "We're here. Seats 2A and B."

"I'm sorry sir, the last call was two minutes ago. The jet bridge is closed."

"Please. My dad died. You have to let us on." D.K. handed her their tickets. "I can't miss his funeral."

"It's okay, boo." Crystal rubbed his back. "She'll let us on."

The agent picked up the phone and spoke in a soft voice. "2A and 2B. A funeral." She gave them a faint smile and hung up. "Pilot's allowing it. Come on." She opened the door, and scanned their tickets. "I'm sorry for your loss."

They took their seats and held hands as the plane took off. Once airborne, D.K. pulled the Delta comforter and pillow out of the plastic wrap, and pushed the buttons on his first-class seat to recline flat. He slept the sleep of a man who'd escaped jail.

CHAPTER THIRTY-SEVEN

⌒

The next day, Roxanne was in the operating room watching her case. A videoscope was inside a patient and a transplant surgeon dissected around a kidney. Their patient, a forty-year-old man, was donating that kidney to his wife, who was in the adjacent operating room being put to sleep by one of her partners. She sat and watched normal vital signs on the monitor when her phone rang. She didn't recognize the number but recognized the Atlanta area code, since one of her friends from residency lived there. She picked up and whispered. "Hello?"

"Dr. Roth? This is Investigator Parker. With DEA Intelligence. This call is being recorded, I need you to know. I've received your tip and had a few questions for you." The woman spoke slowly and with frequent pauses, making Roxanne wonder if the caller was a smoker. "Can you talk?"

"Can I call you back in five minutes?" she whispered as she looked over the drapes at the transplant surgeon.

"Sure. Let me text you the number to video chat. Does your phone have FaceTime?" Parker said.

After she ended the call, she texted Alfonzo. <u>Can someone relieve me for a few minutes, please and sorry?</u>

Within seconds she got her reply.

<u>Sure.</u>

After she turned the case over to one of her partners, she stepped out of the OR and into the empty dictation room in the doctor's lounge. Someone had left a half-eaten banana by the computer and it made the room smell. She closed the door firmly and returned the call via video chat as requested.

A woman appeared on her screen. She had such smooth ebony skin Roxanne couldn't tell if she was thirty or fifty years old. The woman wore a black cap with DEA written in white lettering. She was seated at a computer console and behind her was a conference table with two men working; a long-sleeved black jacket with *DEA Intelligence* in bold yellow block letters was draped on the back of one man's chair. Several maps pinned with thumbtacks hung on the wall next to a large American flag on a pole. A television screen showed a surveillance camera view of an indistinct strip mall.

"Are you Parker? I'm Roxanne Roth."

"Dr. Roth. Thanks for calling back," Parker said. "I'll make this brief. I had just…a few questions before I start my investigation." Parker looked down as she typed. Roxanne noticed the investigator's bare nails; they had beau lines, white horizontal depressions across the nail beds associated with a pause in nail growth. Maybe that's also why she was short of breath, thought Roxanne. Maybe she'd had a pulmonary embolus? A heart attack? Roxanne's street diagnosis never stopped. It was a side effect of being in the medical profession.

"Start the investigation? You're too late."

"Why?" Parker looked from her screen into the computer's camera lens.

"I sent the tip online two weeks ago and have been calling you guys daily. No one answered my voice messages." Roxanne's voice was loud and she held the phone up at eye level. "He was arrested. Assault and possession of an illegal substance."

"So that'll make this easier."

"He's free," Roxanne said. "Released on bail yesterday. No one, anywhere, stops him." The two men seated at the table behind Investigator Parker stood.

"I'll get on it right away." Roxanne watched Parker type on the keyboard. "I was on medical leave and am just now catching up. Can you confirm the address you witnessed the drug dealings at? I'll get a team there as soon as I can. I can obtain search warrants and go."

"Memphis Neurosurgical, on Front Street, downtown Memphis."

"Okay, thanks for your tip. Please keep everything confidential. The less information out there the more luck we'll have. We'll be in touch."

The call ended.

Maybe he was still in town, Roxanne thought, just because he wasn't in the office yesterday doesn't mean anything. It had been less than a day. They might still catch him. She texted Justin before heading back to the OR, knowing he'd check his phone once he was scrubbed out of his case.

DEA on case. About damn time.

She continued to wonder what medical leave Parker had been on and felt guilty for the impatience she'd shown. The poor woman had been sick.

CHAPTER THIRTY-EIGHT

⌒

D.K. felt his comforter slide. Crystal, standing over him, gave him a kiss on the forehead. "We're landing soon," she said. "I watched three movies while you slept. It's so cozy here. They gave me these slippers to wear." She raised her long leg to show him. "And they keep refilling my wine and serving gourmet cheese and warm nuts."

"I have some warm nuts for you." He reached and pulled her close to him.

"As soon as we're safe in the country of the Amazon, your anaconda will be my only concern." She kissed him. "But first, shoes. Shoes, then cock."

There was an announcement in Portuguese on the overhead speakers, followed by, "Ladies and gentlemen, this is Captain Nicolas Oliveria and we will be arriving in beautiful Rio de Janeiro in thirty minutes. The winds are variable. If you could please take your seats and buckle up. We should be on the ground shortly. Thank you for flying Delta."

D.K. watched as the sun rose on the horizon and the city of Rio came into view beneath them. There were blue mountains that he didn't know the name of and a long winding road through them. Clusters of homes and buildings became increasingly condensed. In the distance, he could make out the massive art deco statue of Christ. He was nearly safe, but far from saved.

Their customs agent in Rio, a petite carmel-skinned girl, with her black hair pulled into a ponytail, studied their visas and passports for longer than D.K. liked. He put his arm around Crystal and kissed her forehead. When he spotted surveillance cameras in the ceilings, he decided against a bribe. The agent looked at D.K. "Take off sunglasses. Por favor," she said.

He pushed the glasses off his face and winked at her. She looked again at the passport and held it up to his face. She typed into her computer, read the screen, and then stamped both passports. She handed them back to D.K. and with a flip of her hand, motioned them into her country.

"We're actually in Brazil," Crystal said, squeezing his hand, as they walked through Galeão International Airport. With throngs of petite Portuguese-speaking passengers around, D.K. felt conspicuous. He put his hat and sunglasses back on and crouched as he walked. Crystal pointed to a store near the baggage claim and put her hand out. He gave her one of the Visas and she disappeared for a few minutes as he waited for her.

With new Dior sandals on, and bottles of local palm oil moisturizer in her purse, Crystal was satisfied. D.K. grabbed their suitcase from the carousel and pointed to the *Terminal Doméstic* sign. "Let's go."

"Por favor, senhor." A local man in a blue uniform, with a "GIG" patch on the shoulder, darted toward them. The man pointed to the bag.

"What?"

"Americano." He pointed again to the bag. "Where ticket? How we know it your bag."

"Claim ticket," D.K. said to Crystal. He pulled out the boarding passes and showed the man the baggage claim ticket on the back of his. The man compared the numbers and gave a clap. "Have good trip."

D.K. and Crystal took the escalator to the domestic terminal and stood in line at LATAM Airlines. "We can start in Salvador," he whispered to Crystal as they waited. "It's naughty, like you." He figured Salvador, Brazil, with its underworld of gangs and drugs, would be easier to hide in. There, the police force had enough to deal with. They wouldn't be interested in the tall gringo and his sexy wife. They purchased the next flight out, a two-hour nonstop, that delivered them safely into the lush Bahia region of Brazil, north of Rio.

The sky in Salvador was overcast as they flagged a taxi. The driver loaded their bags in the trunk and opened the door for Crystal. "Please." He motioned to her and spoke to D.K. "Where to, my friend?"

D.K., surprised, said, "Are you American?"

"Mom was." He got into the front seat. "We visited Miami every summer. Where you visiting from?"

"New York," Crystal said. "We've never been here."

"Would you like a short tour? Where are you staying?"

"Show us around and finish the tour at the best hotel in town," D.K. said. "We're on our honeymoon."

The driver shifted into drive. As he passed the favelas, the shanty towns, he pointed them out to his passengers and said, "Avoid there. Only drugs and crime." He drove to his favorite beach. It looked just like a postcard. "Are you hungry? The lady on the boardwalk there makes the best moqueca you've ever had. It's a seafood stew."

D.K. and Crystal devoured the meal. He licked the bowl for emphasis. "That's what freedom tastes like," he whispered to Crystal and she laughed. The beach was immaculate, with soft white sand and turquoise blue water. "I think we found home."

The driver took them to the Church of Our Lord of Bonfim and explained to Crystal what the colorful fita cotton wrist amulets were for. From a street vendor, she bought three pink ones with *Bonfim Da Bahia* written in bold lettering. "You tie them here," he showed her the gate, "and make three wishes." Crystal tied two onto the gate and closed her eyes. She tied the third one onto her wrist.

They drove south along the shoreline to the Fasano hotel. "It's our finest. I think you will enjoy it. The view is spectacular."

At the valet, D.K. tipped the driver in dollars and patted his back once.

"How do I say thank you in Portuguese?" Crystal said.

"Women say *Obrigada.*"

"*Obrigada,*" she said, giving him her manicured hand.

"*De nada.*" He kissed it and bowed to them both.

They unwound in their ocean view suite; for forty-eight hours they ordered room service, slept, had sex, and enjoyed the panoramic view of the Todos os Santos Bay; The Bay of All Saints. After two nights in jail, D.K. fully appreciated the top floor penthouse, and his top floor woman, as he smoked the marijuana the concierge had slipped him. "Let's find some food," he said, after a long drag.

The irony of the saints was not lost on D.K., and he reveled hiding in plain sight as they walked the cobblestone streets, among brilliantly hued eighteenth-century architecture. Crystal received attention from the native men; catcalls and whistles followed her path. D.K. gripped her hand and whispered in her ear, "I don't want you going anywhere without me, got it?"

"Why would I?"

They ate a custard tart, *pastel de nata*, at a nearby bakery. The *cafezinho* they served with it was hot and flavorful. Who knew boiled sugar water poured over filtered coffee could taste so good, D.K. thought as he sipped. "We may be in Brazil, but this is one heck of a Dutch breakfast!" He drank, his eyes still bloodshot from the marijuana.

Back in their hotel, Crystal swam, her hair pinned up as she kept her head above water, as she never got it wet in between salon perms. D.K. reclined in a mesh lounge chair and drank a dirty martini. They had the pool to themselves.

They could hear the samba music from the street party nearby and Crystal stood in the pool facing him. She put her hands above the water and moved her graceful legs in the water as if samba dancing. "We should go out, celebrate our new life."

"And we need to find some blow. That Oxycontin isn't cutting it."

"I bet our concierge will get me some. Do you want me to ask?"

"Yeah. We need a dealer. And get him to book us a table with liquor service at a club, too."

Crystal stepped out of the pool and toweled off.

"When you're done, meet me in our room and give me some more of that juicy ass," he said. As she walked by him, he reached out and squeezed her left buttock, hard.

He couldn't see her wince as she walked inside.

CHAPTER THIRTY-NINE

"That was the absolute worst uterus ever," Roxanne said, entering the anesthesia lounge and dropping the billing ticket into the metal collection box that hung on the wall. The heavy door closed behind her.

Alfonzo, alone and seated, laughed with a mouthful of cafeteria French fries.

"What was the deal?" he said.

"I don't know, took Huntington forever to get it out. I think it was just too large to do laparoscopically, but you know, they never want to give up and do it open."

"Nope, they'll fuss for hours instead of opening."

"Better for the patient. But I was cold, hungry, and had to pee. The anesthesia trifecta." Roxanne rummaged through the refrigerator and pulled out the leftovers from the restaurant she and Justin had eaten at last night after the medical staff meeting. The hospital meeting room had been packed. All fifty seats were taken and about thirty physicians and nurses stood along the walls. Roxanne and Justin had arrived early enough to sit together, and Nick stood behind them.

"CYA," Roxanne had whispered to Justin when an attorney introduced herself at the podium. "They're going to cover their asses now, just watch. Administration didn't listen to the anesthesia department or the ICU teams and now look at the mess they're in."

A seasoned nurse who had been involved in the care of Mrs. Chelsey raised her hand. "I took care of a patient for three straight nights who woke up paralyzed because of him. No one in administration did anything. This was months ago. I called and emailed, begging the hospital to do something," she said. "Why was nothing done?"

"I understand your frustration. However, that case was still under review prior to the suspension." The attorney spoke into the microphone.

"While that was under review, my patient stroked out because of him." Another nurse spoke up. "Do you know what Wallenberg syndrome is? She can't swallow anymore, she can't eat."

"At least they're alive," Roxanne said. "He killed my patient."

The attorney for the hospital spoke into the microphone while raising her hands for silence. "Everybody here is aware of HIPPA and HIPPA violations. You're legally forbidden to discuss patient outcomes with anyone, especially the press. If you want to talk to us privately, work with us, to repair the damage that was done, we would appreciate your input."

"My patient died," Roxanne said. "You can repair that?"

"I meant repair the reputation of our hospital. One doctor does not determine the quality of an institution. Now that Dr. Webb is no longer on staff, do you not want patients to come here anymore? Because unless we all get on the same page about this, that's what will happen. We've lost credibility and we need to regain it."

Roxanne was sickened by it all. She needed to put it behind her and study. "Alfonzo, can you give me a mock oral exam sometime? I'm taking them next month," she said, biting into her cold chicken pad Thai. "It's not going well."

"Sure. Be happy to," he said. "What area you struggling with?"

"Everything. I can't focus with..." she said and waved her hand by her head. "Too many distractions. Maybe I should postpone it." She put the food in the microwave.

"You'll lose hospital privileges without it. Don't delay it." Alfonzo took a drink of his coffee. "You free Saturday? I'll help you."

"Thank you. I know I need to get it over with, I'm just struggling with..."

Roxanne looked up at the television on the wall behind Alfonzo. A mug shot of D.K. Webb filled the screen. "Did they get him?" She bolted to the TV and turned the volume up. "That's Webb!"

"They arrest him again?" He stood and walked next to her.

"Shhh shhh." Roxanne waved, her gaze glued to the TV. A mug shot of D.K. was on a flat-screen. A woman reporter in a patterned A-line skirt and black short-sleeved shirt stood by the screen that displayed the mug shot. "As we reported in February," she said. "Neurosurgeon D.K. Webb was arrested for assault and possession of an illegal substance and was subsequently released on bail. Today his office was filled with DEA agents and police officers executing search warrants." A video played and the reporter voiced over it. Roxanne watched the video, her hand over her mouth.

A black sedan was parked in front of Memphis Neurosurgical, as well as six police cars with their blue lights flashing. A woman wearing a baseball hat with *DEA* on it in bold white lettering carried a box out of the clinic; Roxanne recognized her as Investigator Parker from Atlanta. Another DEA agent was walking a German shepherd around the perimeter of the building. Several other news vans could be seen in the background.

The reporter's voice continued. "The U.S. attorney's office says it's part of an open federal investigation. Teams executed search warrants although no one could comment on the specifics in those warrants at this time. Several boxes of what appears to be evidence were removed by multiple agents around five-thirty Monday afternoon."

"He ran a pill mill. I notified the DEA months ago," Roxanne said, still looking at the screen. "Took them over two damn months."

The reporter continued. "Calls to Dr. Webb's lawyer, Frank Lipman, remain unanswered. The hospital representative where he worked in Memphis told us he is no longer on staff and had been suspended at the beginning of January. Dr. D.K. Webb is still at large."

"A neurosurgeon that deals drugs on the side?" Alfonzo said. "That's a hell of a side hustle."

"Of course he disappeared," Roxanne said. "Justin knew he would flee." She rubbed her forehead.

The mug shot appeared again, this time with *SEEKING INFORMATION* in red letters underneath it. A phone number was printed with the words *Crime Stoppers* flashing. The reporter's voiceover continued.

"If you have any information regarding Dr. D.K. Webb's whereabouts, please notify Crime Stoppers. We will have continuing coverage as this story unfolds."

"What a joke. Now they have Crime Stoppers on him." She threw her lunch in the garbage. "They had that sociopath behind bars and they let him go."

CHAPTER FORTY

D.K. woke as the midday light cascaded into his bedroom. He'd rented a penthouse condo with a wrap balcony overlooking the bay. Situated in front of the Bahia Marina, he had a view of Itaparica Island through the floor-to-ceiling windows in his bedroom. He ran his hand through his hair. Crystal had dyed it black, insisting "the platinum stands out among all the Black and brown people here." She was right, and he would do just about anything to not go to jail. Violent inmates would love his porcelain white ass, he thought. He curled up against Crystal's warm skin. The other two girls from the club were gone; Crystal must have already paid them for their service. He reflected on his night. It had been the raunchiest he'd ever had.

"You hungry?" he said, and rubbed her lower back.

"I could go for a bite." Her voice was still thick with sleep.

After they showered and dressed, Crystal in her white see-through leotard and jean shorts, they walked around the pedestrian promenade in town. It was a different place without the crowds of Carnival. Mostly just the locals were there now peddling to any passing tourist. They bought sugar cane juice from a stand; the man handed the cup to Crystal and bowed to D.K. They walked around the brightly painted homes in the center of town—purple, yellow, blue, the brighter the better seemed to be the motif—and went inside a bar.

A standing crowd of patrons watched the television above the bartender. They cheered any time a man in yellow had the ball. Brazil was beating Paraguay in a World Cup qualifying match. "Their definition of football is so stupid," D.K. whispered to Crystal. "Real men tackle."

When the game finished and the crowd dispersed, D.K. and Crystal got a pen from the bartender and went to the payphone booth. Crystal stood outside the clear paneled door D.K. had closed. It was quiet inside and he dialed Seth's number using the yellow Post-it from his wallet.

"Dude," Seth answered. "What took you so long to call?"

"I wanted to let the dust clear a bit."

"Don't you have internet where you are? The DEA raided your clinic." He could hear Seth chewing gum. "You can't ever come back here."

"Wait," D.K. said. "The DEA? How'd they know?" D.K. turned to look at Crystal. Her back was to him as she leaned against the booth and examined her false nails. "You sure it was the DEA?"

"I watched the whole thing from my apartment window."

"I thought you cleaned the place out."

"I did. I don't know what they found out. But they took so many boxes out, man."

"Did you empty the basement?"

"There's a basement?"

D.K. shook his head. What did it matter, anyway? He was Mr. Chip Conway now, just some gringo who'd moved to Brazil. He wasn't ever going back.

"All right, it doesn't matter. I just wish you had sold that shit instead."

"I sold everything I knew about. I got eighty grand for your bike, even without a title. There's over a million dollars transferred."

"Listen, can you go Snowden techno geek on this and find out who tipped off the DEA? I'm going to make sure the son of a bitch pays. He cost us a lot of money."

"I'm on it, man. I know just the dork who can help. It might take some money and time. Be careful, wherever the hell you are. They're after your ass for real now."

"I'll call you back soon."

A week later, after he dropped Crystal off at the hair salon, D.K. passed a motel painted in bright pink and a parking lot filled mostly with economy cars like Fiats and Nissans. He was on the lookout for a new bike, but so far he'd only seen Vespas. A Vespa wasn't for a man of his status. He walked to the bar to use the only payphone he'd found in town.

A beggar, wearing a bright orange knit cap even though it was eighty degrees out, sat taller as D.K. approached. His clothes looked like they hadn't been washed in a decade. Lying next to him was a similarly disheveled, silent terrier mutt with a black head and a white body. D.K. bent, petted the dog, and spat on the sidewalk near the man's shoeless feet. The man clutched his dog and cursed in Portuguese.

D.K. strode into the bar and ordered an Invicta, a Brazilian micro beer, from the bartender who'd lent them a pen last week. "Hey, man." He made a writing motion with his hand. With a pen and a beer in hand, he went to the back corner, shutting the payphone booth door behind him.

"You figure it out?"

"It took some serious software to break into the DEA tip line," Seth said. "But we did it. Three days and four computers, but we did it. It was a woman. Roxanne Roth."

That uptight bitch, D.K. thought. "Give me Tito's number," he said. He pulled the Post-it out of his wallet and wrote the number down. "I owe you."

Tito answered and D.K. filled him in on the target. "Get her left arm. Tonya Harding the shit out of it, but make it permanent. If I can't work, neither can she."

CHAPTER FORTY-ONE

⌒

The radio alarm, set on the eighties channel, sounded at 06:00 Thursday morning. Roxanne hit the snooze button as El DeBarge's "Oh Sheila" played. It brought back memories of a cheerleading routine from high school, and she smiled at the thought of simpler times.

She stretched herself alone in bed, wiggling her toes, her arms above her head. She had two and a half hours to meet Justin at the airport; he was coming off shift and flying with her to North Carolina for moral support as she sat for her oral board exams. She felt utterly unprepared; she still stuttered and hesitated and lost focus during mocks. This final exam of her training had a twenty percent fail rate but she hoped she could pull herself together at go time.

After she finished packing her carry-on, she took Lyla for a walk along the river. She loved Memphis in April. It was pure resort weather adorned with frilly flowers from blooming magnolias, azaleas, and crepe myrtles. She wore a blue V-neck T-shirt tucked into her jeans. The humidity and heat would commence in May, but the clear sky as the sun rose higher in the east was ideal. There weren't many cars driving along Tom Lee Park at this early hour so Roxanne let Lyla off leash to run in the grass a bit. Lyla pranced and sniffed her usual spots.

"Good girl," she told Lyla, attaching the leash again after the dog had relieved herself. As they headed back to the condo on Tennessee Street, they were alone; the businesses were still closed and there were no pedestrians in sight. Except for one. A man, that seemed as tall as he was wide, with a port-wine birthmark that covered half his face, was walking in her direction on the opposite side of the street. Had he been a patient of hers? He looked familiar. She wondered if the birthmark affected his vision, as it covered his entire right eye. Poor guy, she thought. As he got closer, he seemed to be staring at her. His expression was not kind. She saw a flash of metal in his right hand. She felt anxious and quickly turned in the opposite direction, wishing she had her Mace can with her.

"Come on, Lyla!" she said, pulling on the leash and while crossing the street her walk turned into a run. Lyla's tail tucked under her as she ran with her.

"Hurry," she said, pulling on the leash. They weren't fast enough. She felt a thick arm wrap her waist and lift her. She dropped the leash and screamed until another hand, this one gloved, pressed against her mouth, almost suffocating her. Lyla barked and bit the man's leg. When he kicked Lyla, she landed hard against the alleyway brick wall and whimpered.

"You bitches need to shut up."

Roxanne bit his hand but only managed to taste the leather of his glove. She wriggled and kicked him, but he was a wall. Massive. She felt the man release pressure on her mouth and she tried to scream again. Instructions flashed from a self-defense course she'd taken back in high school. "Fire! Help! Fire!" She screamed as loudly as she could. This time he put his hand across her neck and whispered. "One more word and I break your pretty neck, you hear me?"

Roxanne looked frantically at the empty street as he carried her deeper into an alleyway behind a green opened dumpster. Lyla remained lying by the wall where he'd kicked her, on her side and whimpering. A feral cat ran out of the way. "Please, please don't. I have money. I'll give you whatever you want, please, please!"

"Face it lady, you're screwed." He used his massive body to pin her against the wall then pulled out a metal bar from behind him.

Roxanne put her left arm up to protect herself from the blow, her entire right side pinned to the wall from his enormous weight. A sound. Like a bat connecting with a ball. Her voice made a sound she'd never heard. The pain, blinding pain, radiated through her. She screamed as he hit her harder in the left arm again. Her eyes rolled back and she felt nothing, her mind shut down from pain too intense to process.

⌢

"Sir, you'll have to board now." The blonde agent with an oval face and wrinkled skin spoke louder. "Final boarding call for Raleigh was five minutes ago. I have to close the gate."

Justin looked down the concourse seeing the atrium of stores, but not his girlfriend. He hadn't heard from her since six-thirty that morning. She'd texted Walking Lyla, see you soon.

He called her cell multiple times, listening to it ring and then go to voicemail. He called her home phone, no answer. He could see that she hadn't read the messages he'd sent her on WhatsApp, but he couldn't tell if she'd read his text messages. He also figured her phone wasn't out of battery or it would've gone straight to voicemail. He looked through his contacts and dialed a number.

"Hey Claire, did Roxanne drop Lyla off yet?" Justin said, trying to mask the concern in his voice. "Have you heard from her this morning?"

"I was just calling her. I thought she'd drop Lyla at seven-thirty."

"I'm heading back to her place. She wouldn't miss this flight. She's not at the airport, and she's not answering her phones."

"What time's the flight?" Her sister's voice now an octave higher.

"They're closing the boarding door," he said, as he jogged away from the gate, his bag hung over his shoulder.

"Sir, sir!" The gate agent's voice echoed behind him. He saw a woman with long curly black hair walking his way. He squinted, realized it wasn't her and then came a sinking in his chest.

"I'll meet you there," Claire said.

The drive to Roxanne's condo usually took twenty minutes from the airport; Justin did it in twelve. He double-parked his Jeep and took two stairs at a time, bolting to the entrance. He used his FOB to get through the secure door and pushed the elevator's up button over and over.

Using his key to enter the apartment, he found her carry-on bag and purse by the door. "Roxanne?" he yelled, entering the bedroom and master bath. He looked on the patio. "Lyla?"

His mind flooded with thoughts of what could have happened. He heard the front door open and his heart skipped as he went to the corridor to look.

"She here?" Claire said, as she set her purse on the foyer table, her long straight hair pulled into a ponytail.

"No, and neither is the dog."

"Oh my god. I'm calling the police," Claire said, dialing 911. Tears were welling in her eyes. "My sister is missing." She said into the phone.

"You stay here in case she comes back?" Justin said. "I'm going to go look for her."

Claire nodded at him with her cell phone to her ear. "We need help immediately," she said.

Justin sprinted down the five flights back to the lobby and traced their usual walking route. Maybe she just fell or something, he thought. He would see her. He turned left out of the building, surveying Tom Lee Park from his elevated vantage point. He saw a couple of people walking their dogs along the river and one family with kids in strollers. He darted along the back streets she normally used to return from the park. Then he heard it. A bark. Lyla's bark.

He ran toward the noise.

In an alleyway next to a dumpster Lyla was hunched over, barking, and standing guard by her human. When Lyla saw Justin, she limped toward him, whimpering. Behind her were long legs in denim jeans; the building cast a shadow over her hip. She was on her right side, her head on the asphalt, a pizza box from the dumpster next to it. Her left forearm was mangled and bloody. Long black hair covered part of her face.

"Roxanne!" He screamed and ran to her. He lifted her head and felt her breath on his hand. She moaned. "Roxanne! Baby!"

He took out his cell phone and called 911.

CHAPTER FORTY-TWO

⌒

D.K. wandered by the street vendors selling food under red tents. He bought fragrant barbequed sirloin, fresh off the coals, which were handed to him on a metal stick. The vendor watched with satisfaction as D.K. bit into the tasty meat. After he paid with Brazilian coins he walked further, guzzling beer from a plastic cup.

He found himself across the street from a hospital near the marina. It had the decoration of a red heart on the blue tiled entrance and several words he couldn't translate, but he read *Hospital da Crianca* at the bottom of it. It was a three-story building with a gated entrance that looked more like an American parking garage than a hospital. Still, he looked with longing. He missed the power he held when he put on his white coat and entered a hospital or clinic. Everyone there to serve him, handing him whatever he needed to cure, or kill, a patient. Now he was just another rich gringo.

He walked with a clipped pace and a clenched jaw.

"Is it done?" he said into the bar payphone.

"As requested. You do shit to a doctor, it makes the news. They didn't identify her but say she's in the hospital. I doubt they'll be able to do much for her arm. She's done working like you wanted."

"You screw her too?"

"I had to bolt." Tito coughed. "I wanted to, though."

Mission accomplished, D.K. thought. Now *she* would know what it felt like not to work. To not to be the doctor anymore.

He went back to his apartment, where Crystal was naked and passed out on the bed. He took two Oxycontin off the dresser, followed by a swig from an old beer, and rolled back into bed, gently lifting Crystal so she lay on top of him. She murmured and snuggled his neck. He caressed her bottom.

What could he do now that he was no longer Dr. Webb, he thought. And get away with, that is.

CHAPTER FORTY-THREE

⌒

*D*r. Favaro, the emergency room doctor, knocked on the door then popped her head in. "The ortho docs are back to see you, and your nurse is bringing more Dilaudid."

Roxanne was slumped back in her stretcher with a glazed expression, her blue hospital gown with just her right arm in the sleeve. Her injured arm, exposed, rested on a pillow with an ice pack on the wrist. Justin stood next to her, stroking her hair. He'd just put another warm blanket around her torso and legs.

They could hear men and women in the hallway, footsteps and laughter. The ER's ceiling paging system sounded. "Four twenty-six for discharge, room four twenty-six for discharge," a crisp female voice.

Four men wearing scrubs and white coats entered. Two of the white coats had resident doctor badges on their right sleeves. One guy, who probably still got carded for alcohol, wore a shorter white lab coat with a medical student badge on it.

The shortest surgeon, who was at least six feet tall, spoke. "Dr. Roth, I'm Tommy Park. I think we've done a case together but it's been a few months. The team," he tilted his head to the residents, "told me of your assault. I am so very sorry."

"We've done…a few cases together." She grimaced as she adjusted her hand on the pillow. "You're good, I'm glad they called you."

"Well, after reviewing your films, I need to consent you for surgery." Tommy touched all five fingers on her left hand to evaluate blood flow. "This is a nightstick ulnar fracture. It needs surgical fixation with plates and screws. Can you rotate your arm like this?" She tried to mimic him, slowly and with much grimacing, but she couldn't rotate her wrist. "Let's start the antibiotics right away and get you into the OR. They told me they're setting up the room."

"Did they clear her head?" Justin said. "Her neck?"

"Sorry Justin, I thought the ER team had updated y'all. CT clear, labs clear, no other trauma detected, just this awful blunt trauma to the forearm."

"What am I looking at post-op?" she said. "Am I going to be okay?"

"I'll do my best to get you aligned, but I won't know a realistic prognosis until I'm in." He wrote some numbers on the back of his business card and handed it to Justin. "That's my personal cell. Post-op, you guys call me anytime you need."

"I'm afraid to even look at my wrist," she said. "It's not going to align, is it?"

Tommy gave her a look of solidarity. "It's going to be challenging, I don't want to give you false hope. There's a chance the ligaments and bones are too damaged but we're going to do everything in our power to get you a good outcome."

Alfonzo walked in. "Guys, the team's pulling the trays. Shouldn't be too long."

"Sounds good, I'll see you up there." His entourage followed him out, their white coats cloaking them like a shield. A shield Roxanne wished she was wearing.

"It hurts so bad," Roxanne's said, wiping tears and looking up at Alfonzo. "I imagine it's worse than labor." She held out her hand where the IV was placed, and reached out to Alfonzo's extended arm for an embrace. He hugged her leaning over her stretcher.

"You poor girl, all this pain and no baby at the end of it."

"Are you taking care of me? Tell me you are."

"She-Rox, of course I am." Alfonzo's dimples were magnified by his upside-down smile. "You're my only concern this morning. I gave the board to Sullivan."

"It's throbbing." The pain medicine wasn't doing anything except slowing her speech. "I'm supposed to be sitting for oral boards tomorrow." She let the tears flow. "I was targeted. D.K. sent him. The police won't find either of them. I'm certain. D.K.'s untouchable." Through her tears she noticed Alfonzo's shoes. Bright yellow. "Can you drug me now? Please. It's all too much."

"I've got you covered." Alfonzo reached into the right pocket of his scrub top and pulled out a vial. He searched for a sterile syringe from the drawer behind her stretcher and then drew up the contents of the vial. "I reviewed your labs and chart. I think you deserve a little break from being so courageous." He pushed the midazolam in the IV then patted her hand. "This will help."

⌒

"Hey baby, they're sending for you now. I'll see you in pre-op, all right?"

What time is it? Where am I?

"Justin? What'd you say?" The room was dark. The pain in her left arm hit her at that moment and her clarity returned. *Oh yeah. Assaulted. Broken arm. Port wine. D.K.*

"You fell asleep."

"You sure Lyla's okay?"

"I promise. Vet said she has bruising on her right side but said there's no sign of internal bleeding. He's keeping her under observation tonight but she'll be fine."

"She bit that beast, she tried to save me. And he kicked her."

They heard another knock on the door.

"Hey, I volunteered to transport our VIP to pre-op," Keith said.

"Justin, thank you for saving me, for finding me." She turned her head to face him, but since the overhead lights were off, she couldn't see his expression. She reached out to feel for him. "I don't know what…without you, I might…"

She felt a kiss on her forehead. "I'm not going anywhere."

⌒

Roxanne shivered on the frigid operating room table. Suddenly fear overshadowed logic. *Oh my God. Maybe I won't wake up from this.* She started to hyperventilate.

She opened her eyes and looked around. The blinding overhead lights were all she could distinguish without her glasses. The image of two men in blue scrubs with caps and masks on was blurry. She felt someone pick up her right arm and place a very cold blood pressure cuff on her.

"You're going to feel it get tight on your arm for a second now." Alfonzo's voice was undeniable, as was the feel of his belly against Roxanne's shoulder as he reached to connect the white disposable blood pressure cuff to the monitor. Roxanne heard the cuff inflate before she felt it.

She wondered what Mark had felt like as a patient. She imagined Mark's voice and saw his smile; his mischievous brown eyes were full of light. She imagined him kissing her cheek, and telling her she was okay.

Roxanne's mind took her to the day his life came to a screeching halt; there she was in the family waiting room with his parents as they watched nonstop coverage of Obama and Romney's presidential campaigns on the news. Families were chatting, and kids were running around and nagging their parents. Then she saw Mark's surgeon and a nurse approach them. "He didn't make it," the surgeon said. Mark's mom's knees buckled and his dad caught her.

She thought of Geeta, and Anjali with her daughter, and a feeling of impending doom took hold of her. "What room are we in? Is this OR 9? Is this Mark's room?"

"Rox. No. It's—" Alfonso said.

Roxanne tried to get up. She wanted to see the number on the plaque above the door.

"Roxy, lie down." She heard Alfonzo's voice and felt her right elbow burn from the propofol pouring into her IV site. "Hon, I'm getting you to sleep, you're safe. We're in room fifteen, I promise."

D.K.'s going to kill me in here, she tried to say before the propofol took effect. She became unconscious again for the second time that day, but this time her friend and mentor watched over her, and cradled her head as it fell back onto her pillow.

CHAPTER FORTY-FOUR

They'd spent most of the night at the club's VIP lounge. Velvet drapes that covered the doorway offered them privacy as D.K. inhaled cocaine off the table. Portuguese music blasted, it smelled of sweat and beer, and the main dance floor was teeming with locals. The light show from the DJ's stage shimmered on them. D.K.'s section had several women, all under the age of twenty, dancing and drinking. As he danced with them, one woman in a miniskirt was bent forward at the waist, her bottom pressed against his groin. She had a tattoo of a tree with roots; it started at her ankle and the branches disappeared under her skirt. He pulled her skirt up to expose the top of the tree on her left buttock, a white thong under her dress. He studied it closely and smacked her on it.

These whores aren't doing it, he thought. Because of Roxanne Roth, he'd lost his ability to cut, to injure patients. It was all he could think of. He looked for Crystal. She was nearby, smoking a joint, her jean miniskirt was off, and she was dancing in her pink thong and tank top. He spoke in her ear. "Take whichever girl you want home," he said and touched her thong. "You're my bottom bitch, I'll see you later."

He walked the midnight streets and heard laughter as he passed a bar. He strolled for over an hour, lit from cocaine, until he found himself looking up at the hospital again. He put his hand in his pocket and caressed the Swiss Army knife from his childhood. Maybe he could get past those gates and find an ICU patient on a propofol drip. He noticed a uniformed guard watching him so he waved and walked away. No reason to blow his cover, he thought.

He was just a rich white man with jet black hair having fun in Salvador, Brazil, not a neurosurgeon and fugitive.

When he turned a corner to walk back to the apartment, he spotted it. The bright orange knit cap. The homeless man was asleep on a cardboard box, lying on the sidewalk, in a ripped T-shirt and jeans, with no shoes. His dog with the black head and white body slept next to him, curled under his arm. D.K. felt his heart race as he took in the scene. The side street was empty, no cars were around, no one in sight. He pulled the knife out of his pocket and crept without a sound toward the man.

He bent and patted the drunken man's head. "This will only hurt for a second," he whispered. He took the knife and expertly sliced him at the level of the jugular vein. The man screamed and struggled to get away, but with one sweep of his hand D.K. stabbed his cricoid, his voice box, so he'd be silent. He watched the man gasp for air and bleed for several minutes until he went limp.

It's so interesting to watch people die, he thought. The thrill of it tingled in his groin. He took the man's knit cap off and rubbed the blood off his knife. The dog, whimpering, cowered near his dead owner's arm.

"You hungry? Don't worry, you just went from the street to the penthouse, like all my females." D.K. picked up the dog and petted her. He'd always wanted a dog as a kid, but his parents didn't trust him with animals. "You need a name. How about Miss Favela? Hottest bitch out of the projects?"

He took her home and left her in the bathroom with a bowl of water and some bread. She whimpered and hid under the bathroom sink. He found Crystal in bed kissing a petite woman with caramel skin. He joined their party, his impotence long gone.

CHAPTER FORTY-FIVE

Roxanne was asleep, curled in the fetal position on her stretcher in recovery; Liz and Alfonzo had put her stretcher into the "Elvis" suite, recovery's VIP room. The door had a glass window that faced into the main unit of recovery; she could look out at other patients and hospital staff but no one could see her. Her left arm was in a full cast from her fingers to her underarm. Liz had found pink casting from the pediatric supply room to use, instead of the adult white one.

When she awoke, she saw Nick next to her documenting her vital signs on the bedside computer. Nick wore his hair longer since their late summer night together, and he pushed it out of his eyes, his wolf tattoo covered by his long sleeves.

"I thought I was going to die," she whispered as she stretched out her legs and lay flat on her back.

Nick propped her cast up on a pillow. "You're alive." He tucked the blanket around her feet and laid his gaze on her. "Unless you've died and gone to heaven with me."

She looked around the Elvis suite, a yellow bedpan still in plastic and a Styrofoam ice pitcher were on the overbed table. She shook her head. "Definitely not heaven."

He laughed and reached behind her stretcher and by pushing on a metal bar, he raised the head of the bed forward so she'd be upright.

"Better?"

"Much."

"Are you cold?"

She shook her head.

He took the oxygen mask gently off her face and replaced it with a nasal cannula. He adjusted the cannula under her nose, tucked her hair behind her ears, and said, "I'm so sorry. Can I get you anything at all? Do you need more Dilaudid?"

"My career is over, I'm disabled now, aren't I?"

Justin walked into her room and patted Nick on the back. A get well balloon floated above him, tied to a small teddy bear in his hands. She recognized the bear from the window of the lobby gift store of the hospital.

"Babe," he kissed her forehead. "How are you feeling?" He handed her the bear.

Roxanne hugged it to her chest, feeling the soft fabric as she cradled it under her chin.

Justin nuzzled her cheek and stroked her hair. "I've been pacing for hours," he said. "It took everything I had to not come in your OR."

She hugged him tightly with her good arm and kissed his cheek as he wiped her tears away. "Tommy's confident you'll gain full function back in that arm," Justin said. "It'll take a lot of rehab, but he's optimistic."

"He said I'll work again?"

"He is certain you will work again," Justin smiled. "It's going to be a few hard months of therapy but you'll recover. He actually called it a miracle. Most fractures this bad don't align back in place, but yours did."

She leaned back on the two-inch plastic mattress and exhaled deeply. Her twelve years of training would not be flushed down the drain, all those exams, those sleepless call nights, and the thousands of stressful cases. She had missed sitting for her board exams and she was going to be out of work for months, but she *would* recover, she would work. And once she did, she would find the man that did this to her. D.K. thought he would beat her into submission, that he would silence her and ruin her career. He was gravely mistaken.

CHAPTER FORTY-SIX

⌒

The weather, as humid as it was hot, caused Roxanne's red tank top to cling to her curves after the short walk from the parking lot to physical therapy. She used her good arm to fan herself with a magazine while waiting for the therapist to call her name. Her hair hung in her eyes so she flipped it out of her way and tucked it behind her ears. She wished she had asked Justin to help her put it in a ponytail before he'd left for work since she was still unable to do it herself.

The room was mostly filled with elders using walkers as they limped with leg braces over their knee replacements. She was the youngest patient there most days, and she was weary of it all, especially of her capable therapist's constant good cheer. Everything still hurt her arm. It hurt to bend it, it hurt to straighten it, and it was damn near impossible to curl a dumbbell. She needed to curl five pounds to return to work and get her life back.

It had been three months since the attack and for the past six weeks, every other day, she used a car service to take her to physical therapy, insisting Justin and Claire go about their days. She couldn't drive while on pain medication, which she needed to do the therapy, but she wasn't going to lose her independence too. She often shooed them away, telling them how much she loved them and appreciated them but she was going to have to learn how to manage, the sooner the better.

In the treatment room she surveyed the patients, all at varying degrees of disability. The room had black padded tables with pillows and wedges;

one patient lay with an ice pack over his knee after his session was complete. Another patient was moaning as he tried to lift his leg with the surgical staples still in the incision. She heard an elderly lady fart and Roxanne stifled a laugh. The poor woman looked mortified.

"Let's have you warm up," her therapist said. "Do ten minutes on the elliptical and I'll be back to get you."

Roxanne grimaced, pushing the handle back and forth. She watched as a teenage girl hopped on one leg over small hurdles. She looked cured, thought Roxanne. After the warm up, the physical therapist had her roll a stability ball against the wall, forced her to raise her arm above her head and keep it there, then roll the ball back down. Then she gave her a green strap and had her pull it taut with both arms. But nothing hurt as much as the bicep curls. She still couldn't do it with two pounds. She dropped the weight with frustration.

The therapist reached to pick it off the floor but Roxanne stopped her. "No," Roxanne said. "I got it." Anger swelled inside her. She picked up the dumbbell and did a curl. He will not break me, she thought. She did another.

"Good job! It'll get easier, I promise," her therapist said. "Let's use the strap again."

She opened her fridge and put a meal in the microwave. Every week Claire arrived with a bag of pre-made gourmet healthy meals like Thai beef skirt salad and roasted herb chicken. Claire stocked her fridge with juices as well. "You have to eat well, sis, since you can't exercise as much. It's important to help you heal."

Her medical partners had given her sixteen weeks paid time off and sent flowers and chocolates. Alfonzo texted her emojis and jokes regularly. Most of the time, surgeons were the brunt of the joke.

How do you know a surgeon's lying about the length of the case he booked? He texted. Because his lips are moving.

She texted back. How do you know someone's a surgeon? She'll tell you.

Justin had moved in with her, which allowed Nick to move in with Megan. Wrigley and Lyla seemed ecstatic with the change; they slept in a dog pile on the couch and Justin slept by Roxanne's side, except the nights when he was on call. When she still had her cast on those first few weeks, he'd help her in and out of the tub at night, and would wash her hair and back and breasts. "They're the cleanest they've ever been." She'd laugh and kiss him, her left cast wrapped in a plastic bag and rested on the edge of the tub.

He wanted to buy a gun to protect them, but she was just as insistent the thug wouldn't be back. "We're *healers*, not killers," she said. She was more scared of having a gun in her home than D.K.'s hit man returning. She knew the statistics. Having a gun in the home actually increased the chances of being shot.

She'd been given leniency with rescheduling the oral board exam. "Just call us when you're ready, we'll fit you in," the secretary of the American Board of Anesthesiology said, and had even sent her a get well card signed by the president of the board. Roxanne set August as her goal, and studied when she wasn't in rehab. But she continued to lack focus and confidence.

Some nights she and Justin would visit bars on Beale Street and dance clubs in Memphis and its surrounding counties, searching for a giant man with a port-wine birthmark on his face. "I bet he's a bouncer, what else could he be?" she said. "He guards entrances, I know it." He'd even looked a little familiar to her. She scanned every face. Until one night Roxanne's eyes snapped open. She remembered. She sat up in bed and rubbed her eyes, nudging Justin awake with her good arm. "Honey. I know where I've seen him."

Justin turned to her and stretched onto his left side to face her with his legs touching hers. "What babe?" His voice was deep with sleep. "You okay?"

"D.K.'s hit man," she said. "I saw him last year. Rooftop Peabody hotel. He was there the night Nick and I...met up." She put her chin down.

"*Met up*," Justin laughed. "It's okay, baby."

"He was there. I knew he was a bouncer." Roxanne rolled her entire body on top of Justin as he hugged her close. "Agent Parker can find him now."

He yawned and stroked her head as she lay on his chest.

"Your assailant was employed to protect?"

"Parker overnight mailed me a secure phone line. They think their computer system was hacked." She snuggled into his chest and kissed his neck.

"I don't trust her definition of secure and I definitely don't trust hotels now."

"I'll call her from a payphone. We can get him."

He kissed the top of her head and wiggled her body up to meet his face. He stroked her cheek and kissed her softly, and then with more pressure. "You'll catch him, I know it."

She kissed him back and lifted her right hand up for him to help her take off the Cubs T-shirt he'd given her. "But first I'm going to catch you."

He obliged with a sly grin.

It was hot in the morning, the air thick as they walked to a payphone on South Main Street. Roxanne spoke to Investigator Parker on the secure line and Justin stood next to her, holding the leashes of both dogs.

"October 22," Roxanne said.

"I'll get the hotel security footage and payroll," Dwana said. "If he was there, I *will* find him, but I'll need you to identify him once I do."

"I have to *see* him?" Roxanne said. "How many men are almost six feet tall, nearly three hundred pounds with a port-wine birthmark over the right side of their face? I don't want to see him. Ever."

"I'll need you to," Dwana said. "It might be a line up behind a two-way mirror, he won't see you, but that's less likely. They'll probably have you ID him from a six pack of photographs. The police have your clothes from the attack, they can match his fingerprints."

"He wore gloves," Roxanne said. She felt sick to her stomach. "He didn't leave fingerprints."

"Don't worry about that, we just need your witness ID. That'll be enough to arrest," Dwana said. "Forensics has come a long way, Dr. Roth. They'll match him to the attack."

Roxanne felt an itch on her leg and squashed a mosquito. "I hope you're right," she said, wiping the blood off her leg. "I really do."

CHAPTER FORTY-SEVEN

⌒

*M*ost women on the beach wore dental floss bikinis exhibiting the "bigger the bottom, the smaller the costume" philosophy of Brazil. Unfortunately, only the men in this Catholic country were allowed to be topless, and some wore Speedos to make matters more distasteful. Their banana hammocks were spoiling his view, D.K. thought. He reclined in the private cabana, Miss Favela curled next to him with her black head on his bare chest. He petted her and drank from a coconut the beach attendant had brought. It was curing his hangover nicely. Crystal had returned to the apartment to shower. Today was his birthday; he was thirty-four years old and pissed as hell about it. All of his degrees utterly useless. His work from college to medical school to residency completely erased. He was erased, actually.

But this was still better than being in jail, that was for damn sure. And there were plenty of homeless in this town to operate on. "And I have you, buddy," he told the dog as he kissed the top of her head. He quickly spit out sand from his lips. "You need a bath, girl."

He gathered his backpack and put a retractable leash on the dog. They walked back along the coastline; D.K. gazed at the horizon as a ferry shuttled between the marina and Itaparica Island. He'd been meaning to go, but their nights were so full of coke and sex that most of the time they didn't get out of bed until afternoon.

He entered the apartment and the aroma of Crystal's fried chicken hit his nostrils. She made the batter so spicy he'd have to chase each bite with cold beer but he relished it. His stomach grumbled. He stepped into the foyer and stopped abruptly. He stood motionless, straining to catch the conversation; Crystal was in the kitchen on the apartment landline.

"I can be there at five," she said.

D.K. shut the front door silently and with three giant steps he was in the kitchen, pinning Crystal to the counter. He snatched the phone out of her hand. She cried out in pain as he forced all of his weight onto her, the kitchen counter jutting against her back.

"Who is this?" he said into the phone. The line went dead. He hung it on the cradle on the wall.

"Are you ratting me out?" he whispered. "You traitor?" He punched her in the face. She fell to the ground. "Who was that?"

Crystal cried out and curled into the fetal position, her hand held her jaw. He stood above her. "I said. Who. Was. That."

The fried chicken was cooking on high heat and the oil splattered his face and right eye.

"Damn it!" he said, reaching for a towel. He took the chicken off the stove and rinsed his eye with water from the sink. He wiped it dry with the sleeve of his shirt.

Crystal was moaning and crying on the floor. "Bakery," she whispered, unable to open her mouth wide, her jaw displaced. "Cake. Was gonna surprise."

"Well, that was a mistake. I don't like surprises." He handed her a bag of peas from the freezer. "Put this on it."

She took the bag and moved herself to a seated position, both legs extended, her back leaned against the wall. She held the bag on her jaw.

He squatted, facing her, and took the bag out of her hands. He examined the wound. "It'll be fine. Just don't talk for a few days." He gave her back the bag, stood, and took a piece of the cooked chicken off the plate by the stove. He bit into it. "That's tasty, baby." He held up the chicken. "But maybe you should have some soup instead."

Get that jaw of yours ready to do its job, he thought as he walked out of the kitchen, leaving Crystal on the floor.

CHAPTER FORTY-EIGHT

⁓

Driving from the airport hotel to downtown Memphis, DEA Investigator Dwana Parker didn't need directions. Memphis had been her home until she was twenty-five, when she'd moved to Atlanta to join her husband at the DEA. She loved Memphis. The minimal traffic, the slower pace than Atlanta, the best BBQ in the world. She had blessed memories growing up here, playing softball for her high school and attending Memphis State University. Now that her parents had passed, she hadn't been back to visit her siblings; she hadn't been well and didn't want them to know.

It was six months since she'd completed her chemotherapy treatment for breast cancer. She hoped to never see that clinic again, with its winding staircase and café on the first level. They tried to cheer the patients and their families with a piano player in the open foyer, bright orange lounge chairs, and colorful abstract paintings on the wall. However kind those attempts were, they did nothing to lessen the nausea and dermatitis the chemo gave her.

But all that was behind her now; she was a survivor. The sun shone on her, the radio in her rental SUV was playing jazz, and when she stopped at a red light she looked up at the blue sky. Like she did every day, she thanked Jesus. She was on earth to help good people like Roxanne Roth and she wasn't going to disappoint her again. If she hadn't been on sick leave, she would've seen the online tip and would have apprehended Webb before he could ever harm Roxanne. Her supervisor acknowledged the steel resolve in Dwana's eyes when she told him what happened to Roxanne. He gave her autonomy over the case. "Whatever resources you need, just let me know."

As she walked into the downtown Memphis jail, she adjusted her bra under her T-shirt. It sometimes dug into the keloids that had formed on her chest wall from the mastectomy. The keloids itched, but with every scratch she would thank Jesus for healing her. The scars were just warrior marks.

Using Roxanne's description, she'd successfully found Tito by way of The Peabody hotel's security detail. He was now in a holding cell awaiting arraignment. Roxanne's positive identification would lock him up without bail, she was certain.

Dwana's former high school classmate, Lt. Jimmy Jones, worked intake at the jail, and had squirreled Tito's phone away for her, even unlocking it by using Tito's fingerprint. Jimmy had a device that covered the phone completely and made it look exactly like a police fingerprint scanner. Tito would never know his phone had been breached. Dwana knew what she and Jimmy were doing was illegal, but Jesus would forgive them. She needed to find D.K. Webb and couldn't take a chance of being denied access to the phone by a judge.

"Got you a sandwich, extra tomato," Jimmy said with a smile as he handed her a bag of Chick-fil-A. She and Jimmy used to walk from school to Chick-fil-A regularly. Her mom would pick them up and drop Jimmy off at his house at the bottom of their cove.

"Thanks," she said. "He talking?"

"A stone has more to say."

"I figured as much. How're your kids?"

"Junior's taller than me and a royal pain in the ass." He laughed.

"Like father, like son." She smiled. "You weren't an angel in high school as I recall."

"Payback's a bitch, for sure," he said.

Safely back in her car she remained parked on Poplar Avenue and found the phone on the bottom of the bag. She ate the chicken sandwich, now cold, as she scrolled through the calls. She pulled out her iPad from her purse and began typing into it. Every number, every contact. No one on Tito's phone was listed as *D.K.* or *Webb* or *Doctor*. His text messages were erased too, no luck there. His internet showed no searches. She scrolled through missed calls and recent calls. *Bingo.* She found one international number starting with 55 and she saw he'd received two calls from it, both near the time of Roxanne's attack. Each call had lasted under three minutes. She Googled 55 on her iPad for international phone codes.

After she was satisfied that she'd copied all the information down, she drove to a coffee house and bought Jimmy a vanilla latte and a scone. She wiped her prints off Tito's phone and buried it on the bottom of the bag under the scone.

She double-parked with her blinkers on and walked slowly back into the jail. "I got your favorite," she told Jimmy.

"Always glad to see you. Send my regards to your parents."

"Consider it done." She didn't have to heart to tell him they'd passed on.

She called her boss on her car's speakerphone before pulling forward into traffic. "I've got a number to trace," she said. "Webb's in Brazil."

CHAPTER FORTY-NINE

*Dwana and Ryan, an armed U.S. Marshals agent, were in an unmarked van parked in an alleyway in Salvador, Brazil. In the bar across the street was the payphone where the calls to Tito had been made. Dwana felt jittery but sipped on another *cafezinho* anyway. That was addictive coffee, she thought. She would miss it back in the States, but she wouldn't miss this van.

Men are so gross, she thought. And her whole career, she was surrounded by them. Ryan, asleep next to her in the passenger seat, not only snored during his sleep but farted as well. Fast food takeout wrappers on the floorboard and his bare feet worsened the smell. She rolled the window down and let in the cool night breeze.

Dwana had set up a hidden surveillance camera inside the bar without the owner's permission. She had plugged it into the wall outlet and pretended to charge her phone, then she took the cord and left behind what looked like a wall cube charger. It hooked up to her van's WiFi, and displayed a panorama of the main room. Her colleagues in Atlanta were watching it as well. Again, she was breaking the law, but didn't want to question the patrons or staff of the bar for fear of tipping off Webb.

Her boss allowed her to do the surveillance but gave orders that if she didn't spot Webb by tomorrow, she was to begin asking locals, despite the risks of Webb finding out. If that gave her no leads, she was to return to Atlanta. She had no proof those calls to Tito were from Webb. She was going on pure instinct.

She watched young locals smoke cigarettes and laugh outside the bar. One of them looked down the street and Dwana's gaze followed his. A white man, distinctly tall, and with jet black hair was walking toward the bar. He had a quick stride and wore khaki shorts and a green T-shirt. Dwana grabbed the binoculars off the windshield and focused the lens on the man. It was dark but the street lights illuminated his face. He had an underbite and a dimple in his chin. He'd gained weight and dyed his hair black. Otherwise he looked like the mug shot taped to the rearview mirror of her van.

She grabbed the photo off the mirror.

"Ryan." She pushed hard against his shoulder. "Webb. Look now." She handed him the binoculars, put her cell phone on speaker, and called Atlanta. "We've got eyes on Webb. He looks unarmed. Permission to proceed?"

"Okay, we'll watch the surveillance inside."

"Call local backup, we're ready for them," Ryan said, checking his pistols; one was on his hip and one was strapped to his leg. He put his boots on. "When they're here we'll move in."

They watched D.K. enter the bar. Ten minutes ticked by. Dwana paced outside the van. After five more minutes passed, she cursed. "We should've manned that back exit. They're taking too long."

"Atlanta's watching inside," Ryan said. "We've got him."

The unmarked police car she was waiting for parked on the street in front of them. Two policemen from the local district and the sheriff shook hands with Dwana as she showed them the picture and pointed at the bar. The sheriff spoke English and he had been briefed on his way over by Atlanta staff. The five of them marched across the street to the bar. Dwana was short of breath but kept up. The sheriff spoke in Portuguese to the men who were milling outside and they stepped away with their hands up.

CHAPTER FIFTY

*B*eads of sweat had formed on D.K.'s brow, and the armpits of his green T-shirt were wet. The air outside was the only heat he'd felt for a few days. Crystal had completely shut him out. "Get off me, you asshole," she told him, pushing him away as he tried to kiss her neck.

She'd get over it eventually, he figured. At least for next year's birthday she would know not to surprise him. For now, he gave her the space she demanded. She had been on the balcony reading a glossy magazine with Miss Favela curled on her lap. He petted the dog and kissed Crystal on the forehead before she could move her face away. The swelling of her jaw had gone down but she said it still hurt.

"I'll be back in a few hours," he'd told her, before taking a bump of cocaine off the dresser in the bedroom and locking the front door behind him. Maybe he'd find a girl at the bar, since Crystal wasn't giving it up. Crystal liked pussy as much as he did; maybe another girl in their bed would open her back up.

He nodded to the guys hanging outside the bar and walked in. Great, it's a sausage fest in here, he thought looking around the bar. No wonder the guys were outside. He went to the bathroom and rinsed his face with cold water. He washed his hands and thought about how much he missed scrubbing for surgery. He let the water run down his arms like he used to do before a case. He dried them and threw the paper towel on the bathroom floor.

The bartender waved him over and offered him his usual microbrew. The cold bottle felt good on his lips and he swallowed it down in two long gulps. He was even hornier now, he thought. Maybe he'd go to the club. He stood, reached into his back pocket and pulled out a twenty. "Keep the…"

"Freeze, Webb!" A loud male American voice rang behind him.

"*Todos abaixem-se!*" Another man said from across the room. D.K. watched as the bartender dropped to the ground behind the bar. D.K. reached into his front pocket and opened his Swiss Army knife as he slowly turned his head toward the first voice.

"I said freeze!" The American in a bulletproof vest, whose pistol was pointed at his head, shouted from three feet away. A petite Black woman with a DEA cap stood next to the man with the pistol and said, "D.K. Webb, you're under arrest for conspiracy to unlawfully distribute a controlled substance, assault with a deadly weapon, aiding and abetting assault with a deadly weapon, and felony for failure to appear. Put your hands behind your head."

D.K.'s eyes darted around the room as he tried to envision an escape route. The barrel of the gun pointed at his head blocked the view of the front door. His knife was useless. The three other men in the bar were lying face down on the floor. He felt the local cop grab his right wrist, which forced him to drop his knife, and then his left wrist twisted as cold metal handcuffs tightened around his back. There's got to be a way out, he thought. How the hell had they found him?

"You've got the wrong guy. I'm Conway. Who's Webb?"

The woman showed him the mug shot from her van's rearview mirror. "Look familiar, Mr. Conway? You have the right to remain silent, anything you say can and will be used against you in a court of law."

"Which court of law?" he said. "We're in Brazil."

"Ever hear of extradition, Mr. Webb?" she said.

"It's *Dr.* Webb," he said. "And you don't know who you're dealing with."

The agent with the gun put his pistol back into its holster on his hip and laughed. "Looks like we got our fugitive," he said, and holding onto D.K.'s elbow, shoved him toward the exit. "Keep talking, asshole."

"You picked the wrong country to flee to," the woman said, walking on the opposite side of him. "These officers will have no problem helping us get you back the States to face your numerous charges."

"I get a phone call to my lawyer."

"Sure thing," she said. "You can call whoever you want." Her smile displayed white teeth against her ebony skin. "Once we get back to the States."

The man pushed him into the back of the police car and made him duck his head. The handcuffs cut into him, sliced him, and he felt warm blood trickle at the surface of his wrists. "Damn man, not that hard!" D.K. said. Once he was seated the man slammed the door, barely missing his foot. D.K. glared at them but the DEA woman didn't notice. She was busy texting into her smartphone.

The car started and he was driven away, the cloak of darkness surrounding him. The cops were playing a local pop station; he recognized the artist Pit Bull. With sudden panic, he realized this might be the last music he heard in a long while.

His heart raced, and he pulled his wrists against the cuffs; he looked at the passenger rear door and wondered if these local boys had the wits to lock the door. When the car came to a halt at a stoplight, he twisted his torso and used his cuffed hands to reach for the door release. He pushed with all his weight against the door. It didn't budge.

"*Molhar a mão?* Bribe? I have money…," he said. "*Senhors?*"

The police officers glanced at one another and the driver turned the music up.

"I have a lot of money," D.K. said, louder, and leaned close to the front seat. "If you help me, I can make you rich men."

The cops ignored him and spoke to each other in Portuguese. They were laughing at him. His mind continued to race as sweat formed on his forehead. They were taking him to jail. He'd be extradited to the States; would there be a chance he could get out on bail again? He had enough money to post a million dollars. Frank would get him out. He slowed his breath. Money solved everything; just because these assholes wouldn't take a bribe didn't mean a judge wouldn't. He always won and he would figure this out. And when he was free, he would hunt down and slaughter whoever ratted him out. He just hoped it wasn't Crystal.

CHAPTER FIFTY-ONE

⌒

The breeze from the summer evening air felt good against Roxanne's bare legs under her blue maxi dress, as did the soft grass under her sandals. The Memphis Botanic Garden was hosting the annual Memphis Food and Wine Festival and she'd received two tickets from Brian Armstrong in a get well card. Inside he'd written with a blue pen:

Please accept my deepest apologies for not heeding your warnings. I hear you're coming back soon. I've missed working with you. Sincerely, Brian.

Over fifty booths created a semicircle; she and Justin had received a greeting bag at the entrance with two wine glasses inside. She sipped a Riesling that was sweet and fruity. With her smartphone she took a picture of the bottle the sommelier held up for her. He filled the glass further. "Cheers."

"I'm up by two," Justin said as he waved across the lawn to a man. Their ongoing game ensued. She always knew more people at any event than he did despite his desperate attempts to beat her. People just seemed to remember her.

"Do you even know that guy, or are you just trying to win?"

Justin laughed. "That's Ricky. He's an intern."

The aroma of ethnic foods wafted over them. They walked by the gourmet Mexican booth and waved to the chef, who knew them well from their visits to his restaurant. "I get to count him, he waved to me first," Justin said.

They tried an Indian curry stew too spicy for Roxanne's taste. They drank some more wine and walked toward the stage. They listened to a cover band play an impressive rendition of a song by Prince. Another brilliant soul gone too soon, she thought.

She bit into a cheese toast with a beef brisket topping. As it coated her tongue, she rolled her eyes. "Oh, you have to try this."

As Justin took a bite, Roxanne felt her phone vibrate. She handed the wine to Justin and looked inside her purse. She pulled out her phone and her mouth fell open as she read a text from Dwana Parker.

<u>We got Webb. Thank you.</u>

Relief washed over her as did pride. She'd done it. She held the text for Justin to read and said, "We don't need wine, we need champagne." She stood on her toes kissing his neck.

"Hot damn," Justin said, lifting her off her feet and hugging her tightly. He twirled her around, and her skirt ballooned around her. "You *caught* the bastard."

She laughed and held on tightly with her good arm. That psychopath would rot in a jail cell. She looked up at the clear sky and focused her gaze on the brightest star. She said a prayer of gratitude silently and thanked Mark. Her angel was looking out for her, she was certain.

CHAPTER FIFTY-TWO

⌒

njali wiped the sleep from her eyes. Had the baby cried? She listened and tilted her head. The baby cried again. She got out of bed gingerly, so as not to disturb Kohi, and tiptoed to the bassinet in the corner. At least it wasn't the maximum wail Marie was capable of. "Shhh shhh Marie Geetadita," she cooed into the baby's ear and rocked her. "You hungry baby? Huh, little one?"

The baby was four months old and slept five hours in a row at night, but still refused to take breast milk from a bottle. It was breast or nothing for baby Marie, so Kohi couldn't help with any feeds. But he did everything he could to help Anjali. He was a master diaper changer, beating her by at least thirty seconds. She laughed every time he timed it. "You're such the lawyer." She'd laughed yesterday and kissed his cheek, grazing his goatee. "Too bad you can't bill anyone for it."

"I'd do it a lot slower if I was billing," he said. "Maybe even as slow as you." He'd picked his clean daughter off the changing table and taken her for a run in her Bugaboo stroller, a present they'd received from his deceased mother-in-law.

Anjali, wearing nothing but her maternity nightshirt, carried the baby into the living room, already feeling her breasts let down. They were so big she was wearing a size F. She hadn't even known a size greater than DD existed. She would be grateful when they shrunk back down to her normal B cup, though Kohi and the baby seemed to like her like this.

She picked up the television remote, sat in the rocker, and offered her baby her right breast. The baby latched on immediately. "Aye Aye, not so hard, Dita." She flipped through the channels and stopped on *News Daybreak* as an I-Team breaking alert flashed.

A female news anchor sat at a curved desk while a video of Webb's DEA raid played behind her. Anjali recognized the raid of Webb's office from previous news reports. She sat straighter and turned up the volume, using the remote. "We first reported on Dr. D.K. Webb in February," the news anchor said. "The neurosurgeon was arrested for assault in Arkansas with a deadly weapon and illegal possession of a controlled substance. He subsequently posted bail and failed to report to court. We also reported the DEA raided his clinic and have been on the search for him since. This morning with an I-Team exclusive report, Dwana Parker, a DEA Investigator from Atlanta, spoke with us first. Here's news investigative reporter Jason Cobb with the story."

"Kohi," Anjali called out to him. "Kohi, wake up."

"Thank you, Jennifer," Jason said. The reporter was standing outside a federal prison in an undisclosed location. A petite Black woman wearing a DEA hat stood next to him. "Investigator Parker, thank you for speaking with us. Is it true that Dr. D.K. Webb has been extradited from Brazil back to the United States?"

A mug shot of D.K. Webb with a red banner and the word *CAPTURED* underneath it flashed on the screen. He looked bloated, his eyes were bloodshot, and his hair was jet black.

"Kohi!" Anjali said sitting up. The baby lost connection with her breast and started to whimper. "Sorry, Mariedita, sorry." She held her nipple close to the baby so she could latch on again.

"What's wrong?" Kohi walked in wearing only boxers, putting on his glasses.

Anjali pointed at the television. "They arrested Mom's surgeon."

The interview continued to voice over and the mug shot stayed on the screen. "He was actually deported from Brazil for illegal travel documents. He was traveling under a false name and passport and, because of this, Brazil did not require an extradition hearing. U.S. marshals were allowed to escort the fugitive back to the United States."

"He's in jail. They actually caught him." Anjali reached over carefully so as to not disturb her daughter and picked up a framed photo on the side table by the recliner. Aunt Rekha had taken it of her and her mother at the baby shower; her mom was smiling and had her hand on the baby bump. Their faces were side by side as they had just embraced.

"They got him, Mom," she said softly looking down at the picture. Her tears wet the glass and blurred her mother's face.

Kohi knelt and kissed his wife's forehead. "Anj," he said, stroking her head. "But at least now it's over."

"How are you certain it's over?"

"He's in federal prison for running a pill mill and fleeing the country," Kohi said. "He's a proven flight risk. No judge will ever let him post bond again. That's not even touching all the malpractice charges from patients that will be filed against him. Including ours. He's done."

"If only he gets the death penalty," Anjali said and reached for the landline her mom had insisted they always have. "I'm calling Dad."

Kohi covered her hand with his on the phone. "Let's get dressed and go to his house to tell him," he said. "I don't want him to be alone when he hears the news. And we need to be strong for him. We'll take him out for breakfast. I'll take the day off, okay honey?"

She looked into her husband's deep brown eyes. He was so sensible, so kind. She leaned forward and kissed him lightly on the lips. And wept.

CHAPTER FIFTY-THREE

⌒

The blue morpho butterfly landed on top of her big toe. Crystal giggled watching it, careful not to move and disturb it. It was beautiful, she thought, just like all of Costa Rica. Over the past two months, she'd fallen completely in love with the Ticos, their food, and their rainforest. She'd even taken to zip-lining, laughing and screaming while dangling through the air at forty miles per hour. Up there, flying through the trees filled with howler monkeys, she felt freer than she ever had.

With the clear blue Caribbean Sea in front of her and the Cahuita National Park behind her, she adjusted the strap of her one-piece red bathing suit and contemplated her good fortune; her dog rested next to her, and a giant tree branch shaded them both. She petted the little dog's black head and the dog licked her hand. D.K. was in federal prison for life and she was on permanent holiday.

D.K. had been gone for three days when he'd called her from the States. "It's bad," he told her, his voice panicked. "I need you to pay Frank. Seth didn't answer his phone and I only get this one last call. You have to reach Seth and have him wire Frank the money; Seth has all the codes to my account."

So do I, she'd thought. So do I.

"Sure, baby," she said. "I'm on it. Don't worry about a thing. I'll get you out of there."

After hanging up, Crystal bolted to the bathroom in the penthouse. This was the chance she'd been waiting on her whole life; a chance to live on her own. No more life in the South Memphis housing projects. No more abusive boyfriends. No more whoring around for money and drugs. All of her life she'd had to bend to everyone else's needs. She was going to be the bitch in charge from now on.

She dug through the cabinet under the sink looking for the opened tampon box and went to the couch in the living room. The dog jumped next to her. She dumped the tampons on the coffee table and found a napkin she'd taped inside the box.

One morning when D.K. had been asleep from an all-night orgy, she'd needed to pay the prostitutes. That's when she went into his wallet and found the folded yellow piece of paper. With black ink she copied all the details of the bank account and the access code onto a napkin and returned his yellow paper exactly as she'd found it. She'd buried the tampon box and bided her time. She'd done her research. Brazil was the "Paradise of Gemstones" and she was in the market for half a million dollars' worth.

She packed all the cash that was in the home safe—over thirty thousand dollars—her fake passport, and a change of clothes in a backpack. She remembered to pack some dog food for Miss Favela and realized how much she hated that name. "You're not trailer trash, and neither am I," she said. "Your new name's Misty." She petted the dog and hooked her to the leash. "Misty, let's get the hell out of here."

Wearing the tweed suit she'd arrived in months ago, she gave the wire codes to the bank manager and was able to cash out the entire bank account, a million U.S. dollars converted to Brazilian reals. She hired a car and driver and directed him to take her southwest. She admired the Mantiqueira Mountain Range and Jequitinhonha Valley which held the gold and sparkling treasures that gave the region its name: *Minas Gerais*, or General Mines.

After checking into a hotel in Belo Horizonte, Crystal and Misty went shopping. Diving in and out of H. Stern, Amsterdam Sauer, and Natan over two weeks, she paid cash for emeralds, aquamarines, and the rare Brazilian imperial topazes. She'd read Russia's deposits of the cherry-red stones were already exhausted, greatly increasing the value of the stones she now owned.

With the delicacy and precision of a plastic surgeon, Crystal used a razor blade to cut lengthwise into four large toothpaste tubes. She scooped the paste out, filled the tubes with gems and then covered them with toothpaste. With a delicate hand and a Q-tip, she sealed them back with superglue. Even better than a surgeon, she thought, admiring her work. Her fortune was hidden in plain sight as she smiled at the Costa Rican customs officer upon entering his country. He studied her legs as he waved her through.

Money went far in Costa Rica, and she purchased a two-bedroom home on the sea. Drugs were easy to score but she found herself not wanting them. She slowly cut back until only quality marijuana was in her system. She was done with tricks and cocaine, and by selling off a gem occasionally at stark discounts to the multitude of American and European tourists she'd solicit in town, she would have enough money to live a lifetime here.

She took Spanish classes three times a week and was on the lookout for a food truck to purchase. She would spend her Sundays cooking and selling her spicy fried chicken to the locals. She'd take the truck all over the country, and sell her gems on the side. The Ticos had been so welcoming to her, she wanted to become one of them. Her best self.

She couldn't completely let go of her past. Every week she read the news from the States on her new laptop. She searched "D.K. Webb" for updates regarding his case. The federal judge had rejected his public defender's request for bail, and patients filed an additional six pending lawsuits against him. She watched a video of him in court. He had gained at least thirty pounds, his platinum hair had grown in and was in a buzz cut, and his face was puffy and acne laden. She laughed when she saw him in a prison uniform. Not exactly tailored suits anymore, huh, Dickie?

On the beach she packed up her things, leashed Misty, and stepped into her Dior sandals. She ran her fingernails, free of any color or acrylic, through her natural hair, cut short. The sun peeked out of the clouds and she put her sunglasses on. Yeah, she thought, she was D.K.'s whore no more. Maybe tomorrow she'd try white water rafting. Or maybe she'd drive to Arenal and see the active volcano. Her options were endless.

CHAPTER FIFTY-FOUR

⌒

The air was crisp and the sun was out in Raleigh, North Carolina. Fall had begun and the colorful trees were as beautiful here as they were in Memphis, Roxanne thought.

"You're going to crush it, babe," Justin said, as he opened the rental car's door for her. His freshly shaved cheek brushed against hers as he kissed her. "Text me when it's over. I'll be waiting to celebrate."

"I hope we'll be celebrating." She put her purse strap over her shoulder and hugged him tightly. "You're the best."

She felt a slight throb in her left wrist. Her physical therapist had released her from treatment, congratulating her on her recovery, and giving her home exercises to do daily. Tommy Park had given her permission to return to work next week, and reassured her the occasional throbbing would eventually go away.

Roxanne's stride was shortened; her knee-length pencil skirt confined her. She buttoned her blazer as her heels clipped against the sidewalk. She took the elevator to the testing center on the fifteenth floor, where a woman greeted her, and escorted her to the orientation room. Roxanne surveyed the several men and women also dressed in business suits, sitting with their purses or briefcases on their laps. She wished they could all wear scrubs instead, to simulate real life; they were anesthesiologists, not lawyers. She counted four rows of five chairs in each. If the ABA annual statistics held up, four of them would fail today and be right back here next year to try again. Some knee fidgeting and hair adjusting ensued around the room and no one spoke as they watched a fifteen-minute video summarizing the rules and protocols of the test, all of which they should already know.

"Please come this way." The receptionist led them to a room with wood-paneled lockers. A wall-sized glass panel engraved with *American Board of Anesthesiology, Inc.* and its logo partitioned the lockers from the reception desk. "Leave your belongings, and come this way."

Roxanne took a deep breath and followed her to the exam rooms.

⁓

Refresh. Refresh. Roxanne was on her couch post-call, petting Lyla, with her laptop in front of her. She kept pushing the refresh icon on the ABA website. The board exam results were due. It had been exactly three weeks. She typed her name again into the ABA physician certification status until finally it popped onto her screen. It changed from In the ABA Examination process to CERTIFIED. "Yes!" she said, startling Lyla. She called Justin and heard him whistle. "I knew it," he said. "Tonight, I'm taking my girl out."

After texting her sister, parents, and Alfonzo the good news, Roxanne leashed Lyla and headed out. Memphis was still hot in September but the humidity had broken and the sky was clear. She put her sunglasses on and picked up a freshly fallen white carnation from the side garden before loading Lyla into the car in the garage.

She drove to the middle of town and turned left off of Poplar Avenue and drove onto an asphalt winding road. She parked. The grounds were bigger than she remembered from five years ago. An attendant was mowing the grass. The smell reminded her of watermelons and childhood. She walked slowly, deliberately, until she located it.

Mark's mother wasn't there but her presence was obvious; a floral bouquet sat in a vase to the side. Since the funeral, a bench had been placed as well as a marble gravestone. Roxanne read it for the first time. Mark Dylan McKinney. A beloved son and fiancé. We will miss you every moment of every day.

She placed the carnation on the marble and sat on the bench. Lyla hopped onto it next to her. She petted her. "I'm sorry I haven't visited." She looked around her and saw a family about a block's distance away, otherwise she was alone. She caressed the Tiffany necklace he'd given her. "I just passed the boards. I felt you were with me, rooting me on. I wanted to tell you." She felt awkward talking aloud. "And the Cubs won the World Series. I'm sure your mom probably already told you that. I cried when they won, knowing how happy you would've been. This is Lyla, you would love her."

Lyla licked Roxanne's face and moved onto her lap to get a closer nuzzle. Roxanne hugged her. "I'm dating a good guy you would like as well." She sighed. "But what I would do...to hug you one more time, to kiss you. To tell you again how much I love you, how much I *always* will."

A bright red butterfly hovered in front of Roxanne's face. It circled her head, once and again and a third time before perching on Mark's gravestone. Roxanne was mesmerized. She could almost hear Mark's voice as he read his quote to her from his high school album: "We are like butterflies that flutter for a day and think it is forever."

"That's you, isn't it?" Roxanne said. "Please keep sending me those signs and I promise to always watch for them." When the butterfly flew away, it carried with it the weight that had been with her for over five years.

ACKNOWLEDGEMENTS

First and foremost, I dedicate this book to my mom, Frida Medini. It's been thirteen years since I sent her my first chapter. She read every page and replied, "It's good. Keep going!" Her endless enthusiasm propelled me to write the next page until I found myself with an entire first draft. I would never have completed this manuscript without her encouraging words. I wish every writer such a cheerleader! Mom, thank you for believing in this book, and for supporting me with unconditional love my entire life. I am so lucky to have you. Honey and Tea, Metuka.

I thank my publishing dream team: Copy Editor, Ericka McIntyre, who polished the rough manuscript at the end of this journey and Cassandra Lipp, who meticulously proofread and inspected it. To my talented audiobook narrator, Simone McIntyre, for bringing my imaginary friends to life, and for catching a missing chapter! I cannot thank you enough! My design team, Amit Dey and James T. Egan, I am so grateful for your patience with revisions and your incredible skills. You made my "book baby" look beautiful. Keri-Rae Barnum, Amy Collins, and the entire team at New Shelves Books, thank you for all you have done to pave my path from writer to published author.

To my hilarious father, my Papa Smurf, Dr. Jacob Shiloah; You bring me so much joy! You encouraged my education in writing as much as my education in medicine. Thank you for your ever-present love and support. One day soon, we will travel together again, just not on a cruise! I love you.

I am fortunate to have such supportive friends and family who have read various drafts and listened patiently to me obsess over every last detail; you are the most fabulous crew a lady could want! Thank you so much to my amazing sister Dorit Boxer. It was easy to write Roxanne and Claire's sisterly love and deep connection because of you! Paul Boxer, you are my brother. I appreciate your generous heart, thank you for all you do, you are a true essential hero who gave me courage when I lacked it. My niece Sarah, the other writer in our family, I am so proud of you. Thank you for reading the early drafts, I've kept your handwritten notes from when you were thirteen. You were insightful, even then! My sous-chef, my nephew Jonah, I love you so much. I can't wait to cook with you again. My brother, Dr. Yoav Shiloah, you always leave things better than you find them. We miss you here in Memphis, and we love you, dearly.

My best friend, Manju Chatani-Gada, how many talks we've had about this book over the years! From debating the character names, plotting the villain's next move, to picking the cover art, you never tired of my publishing shenanigans. The other incredible people in my support circle: Monty Gada, Dr. Yula Kapetanakos, Dr. Joyce Roesler, Dr. Leah Windsor, Dr. Stephanie Smith, Heather Huntington, Mary Beth Darrow, Debbie Victor Lewis, the *real* Heather Huntington for letting me borrow her awesome name, Jennifer Gilbert and my work "twin," Dr. Judy Ruiz. You all helped me immensely, and I am forever grateful for all of your input. Dr. Alistair Windsor, thank you for taking my author photo outside during the pandemic, no less!

To my Israeli family, I miss you so much! May we all reunite soon, hopefully around a Shabbat table.

A special thank you to my MAG colleagues; there are so many wonderful people I work with, please know I appreciate you all! I am eternally grateful to have joined the MAG family sixteen years ago. Thank you to the CRNAs I've been privileged to work with who have become dear friends to me: Mary Boers, Teresa Johnson, Mary Day and Crystal O'Guin- who all helped me name D.K. over dinner, as well as Mellie Dzaferagic and Amanda Christopher. I appreciate you so much.

A special shout out to my MAG brothers and sisters: Drs. Chuck Ingram, Ghany Zafer, Ken Kasper, David Leggett, Bennett Bicknell, Jordan Coffey,

Emily Coursey, Shelly Thannum, and "my work husband," Dr. David Reid. You've inspired, encouraged, and mentored me, and I am so grateful.

And to Matthew Arledge, my talented husband, no one cheers louder for me than you do! I could not have birthed this book without your undying patience, input, and support. I would probably still be debating the title! Thank you for accompanying me to so many writing conferences, listening as I read excerpts, and applauding when I gave a pitch at Harvard Writers. There is no one else I'd rather bunker buddy with; I am so grateful I get to come home to you. I love you, Matoky.

This book is in memory of my beautiful cousin, my Hebrew version, Dana Havusha. I hold you closely in my heart, now and always. BCF. Also, in memory of my cherished childhood friend, Jon Kirsch. And in memory of my work "big sis," Dr. Paula Moffett, your MAG family misses you so very much. The hummingbirds still visit your garden.